J Meyerh
Meyerhoff, Jenny
The barftastic life of
Louie Burger : attack of
the girlzillas
$14.99
ocn892701828

First edition.

THE BARFTASTIC LIFE OF LOUIE BURGER
ATTACK OF THE GIRLZILLAS

by **JENNY MEYERHOFF**

Pictures by **JASON WEEK**

○ ○ ○ ○ ○ ○ ○ ○ ○ ○ ○ ○ ○ ○ ○ ○ ○ ○ ○ Farrar Straus Giroux ○ New York

For Amy, Jill, Julie, Sara,
Gary, Brian, and Kevin.
Sisters and brothers, brothers and sisters.
Ain't we lucky?

Farrar Straus Giroux Books for Young Readers
175 Fifth Avenue, New York 10010

Text copyright © 2015 by Jenny Meyerhoff
Pictures copyright © 2015 by Jason Week
All rights reserved
Printed in the United States of America by
R. R. Donnelley & Sons Company, Harrisonburg, Virginia
Designed by Andrew Arnold
First edition, 2015
1 3 5 7 9 10 8 6 4 2

mackids.com

Library of Congress Cataloging-in-Publication Data
Meyerhoff, Jenny.
    Attack of the girlzillas / Jenny Meyerhoff ; pictures by Jason Week.
    pages cm. — (The barftastic life of Louie Burger ; 3)
    Summary: "Louie Burger's dad has to go away for two weeks for a job and
Louie is stuck with a house full of girls. Suddenly, it's makeup, princess dogs,
love notes from your kissy-faced grandma, and heart-shaped pancakes
all the time. How can Louie be the man of the house when it is constantly
under attack by girlzillas?"—Provided by publisher.
    ISBN 978-0-374-30524-6 (hardback)
    ISBN 978-0-374-30525-3 (e-book)
    [1. Comedians—Fiction. 2. Family life—Fiction. 3. Friendship—
Fiction. 4. Schools—Fiction. 5. Humorous stories.] I. Title.

PZ7.M571753Att 2015
[Fic]—dc23
                                                        2014041140

Farrar Straus Giroux Books for Young Readers may be purchased for
business or promotional use. For information on bulk purchases please
contact Macmillan Corporate and Premium Sales Department at
(800) 221-7945 x5442 or by email at specialmarkets@macmillan.com.

ONCE UPON A TURKEY

The long hand of the clock on Mrs. Adler's classroom wall seems to take forty-two *hours* to tick from the two to the three. Thanksgiving break starts at 3:20 p.m. That's only five minutes away, or it would be if the minute hand would move at normal speed. I squirm in my seat and try to hide a sigh.

School hasn't been that bad lately. I only did three embarrassing things this week, and it hardly even bothered me when Ryan Rakefield teased me about them. But I'd still rather be on break than at school. I've got big plans for Thanksgiving break. Comedy plans.

"Before you pack up your belongings, I have two notices to pass out." Mrs. Adler sits on the edge of her desk and holds up two sheets of paper, one in each hand. On the left is a piece of football-shaped brown paper. On the right, a sheet of white paper with a picture of a boy and a girl in the corner.

"Your classmate Theodora has generously invited everyone in room 11 to play football on the morning of Thanksgiving—a tradition from her old neighborhood."

At first I don't know who Mrs. Adler is talking about. Then Thermos stands up, and I remember Theodora is her real name. I call her Thermos because she brings soup for lunch every day.

Thermos stands up to pass out her invitations. I force a smile when Thermos hands one to me because I know she's really excited about the Turkey Bowl. That's what she's calling it. The Turkey Bowl is a great name, but I can't feel genuinely excited about it because, well, it's football. I am not, never have been, and never will be a sporty kid.

I just don't get football. A famous comedian once did a great routine about it. He said football is basically like war. Who wants to be in a war? At least in baseball the object is to go home and be safe. I don't like baseball much either, but it's better than throwing bombs and blocking and blitzing. (Actually, I don't know what any of those things mean, but they don't sound good.)

I hope Ryan Rakefield can't come to the Turkey Bowl because he doesn't think football is *like* war, he thinks football *is* war.

"Can I be a captain?" Ryan asks Thermos as she hands him his invitation. I cringe.

"My dad is going to pick names out of a helmet to make the teams," Thermos tells him. "No captains."

Ryan scowls. Then he reads the invitation and

scowls even deeper. "*Flag* football?" he whispers to Jamal. Jamal used to be Ryan's sidekick, until Jamal realized he didn't have to be around someone so mean all the time. Now Jamal hangs out with Nick and Thermos and me a lot. But he sits next to Ryan in class because Mrs. Adler is in charge of the seating arrangement.

Jamal takes an invitation from Thermos and says, "I can't wait."

"What if the girls don't want to play?" Hannah studies the invitation and wrinkles her nose. "Can we just watch?"

"I guess." Thermos frowns like she doesn't quite understand the question. "If you want to."

I wish I could just watch. I wish Hannah hadn't only asked about girls.

"While Theodora finishes passing out her invitations, I'll tell you about this." Mrs. Adler holds up the second piece of paper again. "Your parents have already received an e-mail, but this is *your* official invitation to Growing Up Night."

As soon as she says the words, everyone looks

sideways at one another and tries not to laugh. Growing Up Night is this really dumb thing they do in fifth grade where you have to come to school at night and learn about armpits and shaving cream. Dad and I have been joking about it for days.

"Next Thursday, a week after Thanksgiving, you and a special grownup will come to school in the evening to learn some important things about becoming a pre-teenager."

My dad told me about his Growing Up Night when he was a kid. He had to practice shaving his future mustache with a Popsicle stick and putting

on fake deodorant over his shirt! I look at Nick, sniff my pits, then cross my eyes. He covers his mouth so he won't laugh out loud.

I look at Jamal and stroke my chin as if I have a beard. He strokes his chin, too, with a big grin on his face.

I look at Thermos and flex my biceps, but her cheeks turn pink and she looks away and finishes passing out her invitations.

"I know this seems silly," Mrs. Adler says, "but I think you will learn a lot. We will show a special movie and a nurse will answer questions."

Ryan Rakefield raises his hand and then blurts out his question before Mrs. Adler can call on him. "Who will answer the boys' questions?"

"I should have been more clear. Thank you, Ryan." Mrs. Adler stands up and walks toward the door. "A female nurse will answer questions from the girls and a male nurse will answer questions from the boys. And don't worry, boys and girls will have separate assemblies. The boys will be in the gym and the girls will be in the cafeteria."

Mrs. Adler stands next to the doorway and holds out the stack of papers. "Okay, you may pack up your lockers. Take a Growing Up Night invitation as you leave."

I hear a bunch of groans, so I can tell that everyone thinks this event is as stupid as I do. You don't have to learn how to grow up. It just happens. But it doesn't happen when you are in fifth grade, so I don't know why we have to learn about it now. The only good part about it is I get to go with my dad. I know we'll be cracking up harder than if we were watching Lou Lafferman. My dad told me when he was a boy, he and his friends joked that they would try to grow mushrooms instead of mustaches.

I open my locker and start shoving as many things into my backpack as I can: my gym shoes, which smell like old broccoli; two half-empty water bottles; an old flyer from the school talent show; a Charlie Chaplin hat; and five hundred crumpled pieces of paper shaped like a strange bird's nest. School breaks are pretty much the only time I remember to bring stuff home.

I'm so engrossed in locker archaeology that I don't notice Ryan Rakefield slithering up behind me. That is, I don't notice him until I hear him hiss at Thermos. "Where will *you* go on Growing Up Night? The gym or the cafeteria? They should have a third room for freaks."

Thermos slams her locker shut, knocks past Ryan, and tears out of the hall without even saying goodbye. We all know that Ryan is a bouncing jerkball and we shouldn't pay attention to anything he says, but sometimes that's easier said than done. I don't blame Thermos for leaving.

Ryan turns to me. I used to be his favorite teasing victim, back when I thought Ryan's opinion actually mattered. Now that I know it doesn't, he can't get as much enjoyment from making my life miserable. But he still tries.

"You probably need the third room, too. You throw like a girl."

I stand up straight and look Ryan right in the eyes. "Thank you for sharing your perspective with

me. It's always interesting to see the inner workings of your mind."

Ryan tries to muster up another insult. His eyes roll back in his head and I can practically *see* his brain trying to think. Ryan opens his mouth just as the bell rings. At first, it looks like the *brrrinngg* is coming from inside him. I imagine Ryan clamping a hand over his lips wondering how he produced such a strange sound. I can't wait to go home and draw a picture of it in my comedy notebook. Just thinking about it makes me start laughing.

"You are so weird." Ryan shakes his head and walks away.

I shut my locker and take a deep breath of freedom. No more school for four whole days! Nothing can spoil Thanksgiving vacation.

THE MAN OF THE HOUSE

I have big plans over break. Sure, I'm going to hang out with my friends, and I'm going to eat a lot of Fluffernutters. Those things go without saying. But I am also going to watch the *Lou Lafferman Day-After-Thanksgiving-Be-Thankful-You-Don't-Have-to-Watch-This-Stuff* marathon. And I'm going to decorate the garage with new comedy posters—posters for my future comedy shows. And I'm going to write fresh material—so I have something to say at my future comedy shows. And I'm going to prank my sisters and I'm going to, I don't know, do whatever I want for four days. It'll be great.

Oh! I almost forgot. My dad and I are going to film my next viral video. I won't need posters or fresh material if no one's ever heard of me, so my videos are my ticket to a life of comedy. I've already had two videos go viral. The first was a video of me accidentally barfing onstage at my school talent show. The second was a video of me spoofing the Three Stooges using my dad's cool junk-art Halloween decorations. Who knows, maybe my next video will get a million hits.

Ruby and I say goodbye to Nick and Henry in front of our house, then they go to their house and Ruby and I go inside to put away our backpacks on the hooks by the door. Then we head out to the garage to find my dad. Most families park cars in their garage, but in the Burger family, the garage is one-half junk-art studio (that's my dad's half) and one-half comedy club (that's my half). The name of my club is the Laff Shack.

Since there are three girls in my family (one mom and two sisters), the garage is the only place with nothing girly. My dad calls it our man cave. My dad is on the art studio side and he's packing all of his art supplies into big plastic bins.

"Good idea," I tell him. "If we clear everything out of here it will be the perfect studio for my next video. I've been thinking, maybe we should make one connected to Growing Up Night. We could call it *Male-Bonding Time* and you could teach me how to shave my mushroom. We could attach mushrooms to my face and I could pretend to shave them off with a spatula. Then you could show me how to use them in an omelet."

I really like my idea, but Dad scrunches up one side of his face.

"What? You don't like it?"

"I like it," he says. "But I'm clearing the garage for another reason."

"You're not quitting, are you?" When my dad first started being a junk artist, after he lost his job as a businessman, he almost quit. Being a junk artist is really hard, especially since no one pays you.

Dad lifts a coffee can full of paintbrushes into a box and wags his eyebrows. "I'm not quitting, I'm working."

He stops packing, picks Ruby up, and spins her around in the air. "Hee-hee!" he shouts. "I'm working!"

"Yay!" Ruby spreads her arms out wide. "I'm a flying unicorn!"

"What do you mean 'working'?" I ask.

My dad puts Ruby back down on the floor. She wobbles a little bit, then falls into the table. "The garage is dizzy."

Dad helps Ruby sit down on the floor, then he turns to me and grins. "I mean, I've been commissioned. Someone hired me to create a one-of-a-kind sculpture. They are going to *pay* me to create a one-of-a-kind sculpture. And it's all thanks to you and the video you posted of my Halloween decorations."

A warm wave crashes over my chest and I feel the corner of my mouth tugging up in a half smile. "It is?"

"You bet." My dad throws his arm around my shoulders and pulls me close to his chest. He smells like a mix of Lever 2000 and paint thinner, so

I wriggle away and butt my head against his stomach.

When my dad first started being an artist, no galleries would buy his work and he got pretty sad. My parents fought about money a lot because my dad's salary was zero. But if people are going to start hiring my dad to do art—and if that's because of my video—then, basically, I fixed everything. My comedy saved my family. I puff out my chest. I'm like a hero. Barftastic.

Barftastic is my catchphrase, by the way, and it probably doesn't mean what you think it means. In my book barftastic is as good as it gets!

I smile at my dad. "Who knows what my next viral video will do. Maybe it will get you a hundred more jobs. Maybe you'll become a millionaire. We better get started."

Dad steps behind his worktable and loads his soldering iron into the big plastic bin. "The thing is, Louie—"

"If you get a million dollars, can I get the new

Magical Mystery Unicorn Mountain Hideout for a Thanksgiving present?" Ruby is now lying on the floor with her eyes closed.

I nudge her with my toe. "There's no such thing as a Thanksgiving present, Ruby." I roll my eyes.

"Then I will get it for a present when Daddy comes back from his vacation."

Now I twirl my finger in the air next to my ear, the universal sign for when someone is cuckoo. "Dad isn't going on vacation. We are on Thanksgiving break from school, but that doesn't mean we're going anywhere. It's the opposite. We're staying home and doing cool things like making my next viral video."

Ruby sits up and opens her eyes. She points at the big box on the table. "Then why is Daddy packing?"

I look at the box, then I look at my dad, who has a funny expression on his face. "Dad?"

He puts the hammer he was about to pack onto the table, then runs his hands through his hair.

"The important thing is that I will be here to celebrate Thanksgiving and we can make a video when I come back."

"Come back from what?" I step away from the art studio and sit in one of the folding chairs in my comedy club.

"From making the sculpture. The job. The people who hired me are with a public library in Pennsylvania. I have to go there to make it. Library visitors will get to watch me work, and then when I'm done, the library will keep what I make." Dad tries to smile when he says this, like it's still the same happy thing we thought it was a minute ago, but a minute ago he was creating art at home. Now, he's leaving.

"How long will you be gone?" I ask. The question pulls me down like wet clothes. "Can we make the video before you go?"

My dad squints one eye, wrinkles the side of his mouth, and shakes his head. "I'm estimating it'll take at least two weeks. And I don't think I'll have time to work on your video before I go. The drive takes fifteen hours. I'm leaving Friday since I'm going to split the driving over two days."

Two weeks? I know it's not really that long, but for some reason the words make my chest feel hollow.

My dad used to work in an office. He was gone all day and I only saw him at dinnertime and on weekends, but he *never* went on vacation without us. And lately it's been my mom who goes to work during the day and my dad who's always home. I've gotten used to having him around.

If he gets more jobs, then he'll be gone even more. He might wind up traveling all the time. We'll only see him once a month or so. It'll be like he doesn't even live with us anymore.

"Is Mom going to stay home from work for two weeks?" I wonder if she's allowed to do that. I've never had a substitute for that long unless my teacher had a baby. "Is Ari going to babysit us every morning, because that is totally unfair. I'm too old for her to be my babysitter."

"I think Ari is a good babysitter, but Louie is even

bester because he plays Magical Mystery Unicorns."
Ruby finds the box of unicorns my dad keeps in the
garage. She lines them up in a spiky parade.

Dad walks around the table and sits in the folding chair next to mine. "You really need a haircut,"
he says, ruffling my hair with his fingers.

"I like it long. It's distinctive."

Dad looks doubtful, but he says, "Grandma and
Grandpa are coming for Thanksgiving, and when
I leave, Grandpa will fly home, but Grandma will
stay and help take care of you and your sisters until
I get back."

"Grandma? But she's always getting lipstick
kisses on me, and talking in funny voices and
trying to make me sing and dance with her. What
about male-bonding time? What if I need you for
something?"

"Your mom and Grandma will help you with anything you need, and you and I can bond on the computer. The whole thing is going to go by much faster
than you think."

"We can bond on the computer?" I ask, and when

my dad nods his head, the tight ball of my stomach loosens a little bit. But then I think of one more thing. "Growing Up Night! Who's going to take me? Grandpa?"

Dad wrinkles his forehead and presses two fingers against his chin. "I forgot about that. Hmmm. Grandpa will be gone, so he can't take you. Maybe Mom can take you."

I exhale hot air through my nostrils. *"Mom?"*

"Or maybe someone else. Don't worry. We'll figure something out."

Whenever grownups say "we'll figure something out," it means something bad is going to happen, but they'd rather tell you about it later. Growing Up Night is already weird and uncomfortable and dumb, but at least Dad and I could have laughed about it. Growing Up Night without my dad is a torture sandwich with extra-sour pickles.

"I know it won't be easy, but this could be fun for you, Louie. You are going to be the man of the house when I'm gone. Your mom will need lots of help. Volleyball tryouts start on Monday and then practices start up right after. Mom will get home a lot later than usual. I'm counting on you to take charge and take care of everyone. Think you can do it?"

I consider my dad's words. Part of me thinks being the man of the house sounds kind of cool. Especially if I get to boss Ari around. Another part of me isn't too sure. Why does everything have to be about growing up all of a sudden?

NOW, ARI—YOU'RE **SURE** YOU'RE SORTING BY **CHARACTER**, THEN **TITLE**, THEN **ISSUE NUMBER**?

"If I can't do it, will you stay home?" And never get more jobs like this.

My dad smiles sadly and shakes his head. "I know you can do it, Louie."

"I guess I don't have much choice," I say. I know my dad thinks I can do it, but I don't think I can at all. Dad helps me with a million things every day. How am I supposed to go for two weeks without him?

PUMPKIN PIE STADIUM

The next morning, I finish double knotting my gym shoes, then take a look at myself in the mirror near the front door. It's Turkey Bowl time.

"It was nice knowing you," I tell my reflection. "If you get smushed, maimed, or creamed today, at least you've already accomplished your goal of being on TV."

Ari bumps my shoulder as she walks by me on her way to the kitchen. "You are so weird. You're just going to play football. It's not like you're going to war or anything."

I give myself a knowing look in the mirror. That's what she thinks. "I prefer other activities to sports. Activities that don't cause broken bones, for example."

Ari rolls her eyes. "You are not going to break a bone from playing flag football. Oh look!" Ari points out the window next to the front door. "They're here!"

At first I think she means Nick and his mom since they are driving me to the Turkey Bowl, but when I look out the window I see my grandma's crazy pink car pulling into our driveway. She won it from selling makeup. That's her job. Makeup Lady.

"Mom! Dad!" I shout. "Grandma and Grandpa are here!"

In the next minute, my parents have come to the door and my grandparents have come inside, with their little white puffball dog, Princess. Princess is wearing a fuzzy pink sweater and a pink bow on each ear. My grandmother kisses her lipstick all over my forehead, and everyone hugs everyone else. Then she picks up her dog and makes it wave a paw at us, saying, "Shay hello. Prinshesh! Shay hello!"

Grandma always talks in that crazy voice around Princess.

I wave to Princess, then I see Nick waving to me from across the street.

"Gotta go!" I say.

"Wait!" My grandpa hands me a new whoopee

cushion. "I got a good one for you. What did the math book say to the science book?"

"I give up." I hold up one finger to Nick so he'll know I'm leaving soon.

"Boy, do I have problems." Grandpa slaps his knee. "Good one, eh?"

Grandma presents Ruby with a sparkly unicorn diary, and she gives Ari a tiny bag with three lip glosses in it. Princess barks. Although maybe it's too squeaky to be called a bark. Princess *yips*.

I start to turn the doorknob, but Grandma puts her hands on my shoulders and takes a long look at me. "You need a haircut." She twirls her fingers through my curls. "Such a waste on a boy!"

"It's not a waste. A comedian needs a signature look." She laughs and tries to kiss me again. I duck my head out of her reach. I should have left when I first saw Nick. "I gotta go," I tell everyone.

"Where's the fire? We just got here," Grandpa says.

"Louie's going to a friend's house for a Thanksgiving Day football game," my mother explains.

My grandfather beams and socks me in the arm. "Attaboy! I knew you'd come around."

Grandpa has been trying to get me to like football ever since he gave me a stuffed football on the day I was born. Nick waves at me again, so I don't really have time to explain that I haven't come around. And never will.

"Well, I should go."

"Sure wish I could see you play." My grandfather clamps his hand on my shoulder.

"What a wonderful idea," Grandma says. "David, why don't you and Gary take Louie to the game. And Ruby, too. Then I can help Laurie get everything ready for Thanksgiving."

I shake my head. "It's not a real game."

"I don't need help, Mom," my mom begins.

"Don't worry. I won't be in your way," Grandma answers. "I'll just be there to make sure the turkey doesn't get dried out like last—"

"Well, I guess that's settled," Dad interrupts, then he opens the door and shouts across the street, "Tell your mom we'll drive, okay?"

Nick nods and runs back into his house.

"I don't even know if I'm going to play. I might just watch."

"Then we'll watch you watch," Dad says.

"That's crazy talk," says Grandpa. "You can't just watch. You gotta get in there. Get dirty."

When we arrive at Thermos's house, there is a big football-shaped balloon attached to her mailbox and a sign that says:

Pumpkin Pie Stadium is in the backyard.

Grandpa leads the charge up the driveway while I hang back. I wish this football game would be like the one in the classic Marx Brothers movie *Horse Feathers*, where Harpo ties an elastic string onto the football so it will bounce back to him and make it easy for him to catch it. He also drops banana peels all over the field to make the other team's players fall down. It is barflarious, but I have a feeling Thermos won't be playing by comedy rules.

In the backyard, Thermos and her dad have spray painted the grass with white lines and numbers so it looks like a real football field. They stand in the center surrounded by kids and parents, mostly dads. Mrs. Adler is there, too. At each end of the field is a giant white structure made out of plumbing pipe. I know they are for kicking the ball through, but I forget what they are called. There are lawn chairs set up along one side of the field. A particularly cozy-looking red one is calling my name, but Thermos sees me and Nick and jogs over to say hello, so I can't sneak off and sit down.

"The game's going to start in one minute. I was worried you guys weren't coming," Thermos says.

"Of course we were coming," says Nick.

"We had a grandpa delay," I explain.

Thermos looks confused, but before I can explain, her dad makes an announcement into a bullhorn.

"Gather 'round, everyone, we are about to pick teams. Parents and grandparents are welcome to watch from the sidelines—there's coffee and hot cocoa on the patio—or you are welcome to play. Who says kids get to have all the fun?"

Mr. Albertson is wearing a black-and-white-striped shirt and black pants, so he looks like a referee. He's got a whistle around his neck. What is it with sports and whistles? He blows it once and makes another announcement. "Will everyone who isn't playing please exit the field?"

I start to walk away, but when I see the look on Thermos's face, I stop. "Kidding! I was kidding."

We walk to where Thermos's dad stands with a football helmet filled with strips of paper containing our names. My grandfather spots me from the other side of the group and edges his way over. "I couldn't convince your dad to play. I hope you and I are on the same team."

I look longingly at my dad snuggled into the red chair with Ruby and a blanket on his lap. They are sharing a warm drink. He lifts his cup to me, like he's toasting the game. Ruby shouts, "Go, Louie!"

All around me, players divide up on either side of the field as Thermos's dad calls their names. He assigns the kids first, and I start to think that maybe the day won't be terrible when I realize that Nick, Thermos, and Jamal are on my team but Ryan is not. We high-five, and I only miss one hand.

When all the kids have teams, Mr. Albertson

divides the adults. There are six of them. Grandpa gets put on the other team. He looks at me and shrugs. Then he says, "Take it easy on me, okay?"

I laugh but secretly I hope *he'll* take it easy on *me*. He coaches high school football in Michigan where he is also a math teacher. What if I do something embarrassing like run the wrong way or pass to the wrong team or tell someone to take a three-point shot when there are no shots in football?

Thermos's uncle Joe is on our team, and when he joins our huddle, he high-fives all of us and says to me, "Good for you for playing." He must have noticed the way I was staring at the lawn chairs.

Thermos's dad hands each of us an orange Velcro belt with two fabric flags. After we put on our belts, Thermos wins the coin toss and decides that our team will kick off first. Jamal makes the kick and I stand way in the back and off to the side. I plan to fake my way through the day.

"Don't be shy," Uncle Joe tells me. "You're allowed to get in there."

"Uh, okay," I tell him.

Grandpa catches the ball and starts to run up the field. Ryan Rakefield runs right next to him, and whenever anyone tries to grab Grandpa's flag, Ryan shoos their hands away, until finally Thermos nicks one. Everyone on my team rushes over to Thermos to pat her on the back. I head over, too, but on my way I notice my grandpa high-fiving Ryan Rakefield.

Ryan is actually laughing and smiling.

On the next play, Grandpa passes the football to Ryan. Ryan runs right at me, so I grab his flag—I feel it between my fingers. I yank and start celebrating. I stopped Ryan Rakefield! I run toward my teammates for a high five, but they are looking behind me and shaking their heads. Ryan is spiking the ball in the end zone. With both flags still attached to his belt.

My grandpa runs over to Ryan. As he breezes by me he shouts, "Don't worry. We all get a case of butterfingers now and then." Grandpa and Ryan fist-bump in the end zone.

I shuffle over to my team and they all tell me not

WHOFF

to worry about it. Uncle Joe boings one of my curls and tells me he's proud of me for trying, but everyone else has that deflated look people get when they are losing. I decide then and there, I am going to score a touchdown or catch a flag or do something right during this game.

After an hour, I've passed the ball to Mrs. Adler twice, even though she's on the other team, knocked over Mrs. Albertson's coffee, even though she's on the sidelines, and caught the ball once, but dropped it, so Thermos's dad called it a fumble. Uncle Joe didn't even say "good try."

Thankfully my team can manage without me. Thermos and Jamal both score touchdowns, and Nick catches my grandpa's flag right before he scores. The score is 24 for us and 28 for the other guys.

The game is nearly over. I can't decide if I should continue to perform my important job of staying out of the way, or if I should try to redeem myself. I've nearly decided on staying out of the way when Ryan Rakefield jogs over to me. I figure he's going to say something nasty about my football skills, so I get my comeback ready. I'm going to say, "Goopen floopen flob."

But he doesn't insult me. He jogs right past me as if he didn't even notice me. I turn around and watch him chest-bump my grandpa.

I don't think Ryan Rakefield has ever walked by me without teasing me before. I'm so shocked I barely even notice when Thermos passes to Jamal and we score another touchdown and the game is over. My team won, but I don't celebrate with them because Ryan is hugging my grandpa, and my grandpa is giving Ryan a noogie. Grandpa loves to give noogies, but before today he only ever gave them to me. Never to Ari or Ruby.

I guess now he gives them to Ryan, too.

"We did it!" Thermos's uncle Joe jogs over to me with his hand in the air. I tear my eyes away from Grandpa and give Joe a high five. "This is Theodora's aunt Lisa." He points to the lady next to him. She has short hair and is wearing cargo pants and a football jersey. She doesn't look like an aunt. She looks more like an uncle. But the more I think about it, the more I guess she looks exactly how I'd imagine *Thermos's* aunt to look.

Joe puts his arm around me and says, "You, Lisa, and Theodora should start your own football team. You guys would be awesome."

Why would I start a football team with Thermos and her aunt? I don't even like football. I try to smile politely since I don't want to tell him his idea is pretty dumb.

"I bet you could convince a bunch of the other girls in your grade to play, too!"

He seems really excited about this idea, but it makes no sense. Why would I want to convince the *girls* to play?

I try to keep the polite smile on my face, but I can feel it slipping away because Uncle Joe's suggestion is so strange and confusing. Why doesn't he tell Jamal to do that? Or Nick? They obviously like football way more than me.

"Don't get me wrong. I think it's awesome to play

with the boys, but sometimes you girls just need to
do your own thing, too, right?"

I have to repeat Uncle Joe's sentence in my head
a bunch of times before I understand. Girls? *You*
girls? Wait a minute. Uncle Joe thinks I'm a girl!

I want to peel back Thermos's grass and slide
under it like a blanket. "I'm . . . I'm not . . ." The
words tangle my tongue.

Aunt Lisa's eyes go wide. She grabs Joe's arm and shakes her head. Uncle Joe's face turns so red it's almost purple. "I'm sorry," he says. "I don't know what I was thinking."

I don't know what to answer. I can't tell him it's okay, because it's definitely not okay. I want to scream at him, but that's probably not okay either. Then I notice a lady in an apron marching straight across Thermos's backyard and my attention is distracted. She heads toward Ryan and Grandpa. They both startle when the lady grabs Ryan by the back of his shirt and starts screaming. "I told you to be out front at noon! I don't have time to wait for you all day. If you can't be where you're supposed to be, you can stay home with your lazy brother!"

She turns and stamps back toward the street and Ryan follows her, staring at the grass. Everyone watches silently. Finally Mr. Albertson makes another announcement into his bullhorn: "Cookies are served."

Twenty people pounce on the cookie tray Thermos's mother carries, like the whole thing with

Ryan never happened. I zoom away from Aunt Lisa and Uncle Joe like cookies are the most important thing I ever heard of. I feel a little bad for Ryan, but I'd rather get yelled at in public than have someone think I'm a girl. I wonder if anyone overheard Uncle Joe. What if Joe and Lisa tell Thermos? I wish Thermos never had the idea for a Turkey Bowl.

Grandpa finds me, gives me a hug, and breaks off half of my oatmeal raisin cookie for himself.

"Hey! That's my favorite flavor, too!" he says.

I don't tell him that I picked it by accident because I couldn't think straight. I never eat oatmeal raisin cookies because I don't like to be surprised by raisins mid-bite. But today, I want my grandpa to think I'm the kind of boy who loves oatmeal raisin cookies. I take a big bite, wincing a little when a raisin squishes between my teeth.

"I'll work on your passing with you tomorrow morning if you want." Grandpa takes a bite of his cookie, too. "Everyone should know how to throw a football. It's a lifelong skill. Your mom throws one of the best spirals I've ever seen."

One day of playing football is more than enough for me, but I'm not sure how to say no to my grandfather. If I say no, he might invite Ryan Rakefield over to play. And maybe if I don't learn how to play football, *everyone* will start thinking I'm a girl.

We meet my dad, Nick, and Ruby in the front yard, and Thermos and her parents thank us for coming.

"It was really nice of you to host this," my father says. "It doesn't interfere with your Thanksgiving?"

"What's Thanksgiving without football?" Thermos's dad says.

"Well, I could live without football." Mrs. Albertson chuckles. Thermos rolls her eyes. "But what's Thanksgiving without a houseful of people?"

"We had a great time." My grandpa shakes hands with them both, then he wraps an arm around my shoulders. "We'll make a player of this one yet."

"Louie doesn't like football," Ruby tells my grandpa. "He doesn't like boy stuff."

Mr. and Mrs. Albertson chuckle, but their

laughter sounds kind of nervous. I look at Thermos. She's got her eyes fastened on a cardinal in a tree across the yard.

"That's not true! I *only* like boy stuff. Just not all boy stuff. There's a difference."

Everyone nods at me, but I can't tell if they really believe me. Nick and I say thank you again, and as we walk back to the car, I feel like I have to convince my grandpa more than anyone.

"I like comedy," I remind him. "That's a boy thing. And I like disgusting things, like boogers and barf."

We get into the car and Ruby says, "And you like Magical Mystery Unicorns."

Grandpa clears his throat and turns on the radio. "Let's see if we can get the game."

I lean over to Nick and whisper, "I only play unicorns with Ruby. I don't actually like it."

"Right. I know that," he says. But he doesn't look me in the eye.

I turn to the window and my curls swing around and brush my cheek.

That's it. I'm getting a haircut.

HAIR TODAY, GONE TOMORROW

After we drop Nick off, I ask my dad to take me to Super Scissors. Luckily I get the last appointment of the day. They close early on Thanksgiving. When I'm all settled in the barber chair with the giant smock practically strangling my neck, I tell the barber to make it short. Really short. Curls might be funny, but they're not worth getting called a girl. The barber slides a pair of clippers over the back of my head. Each time a clump of curls falls to the ground, I feel a little pang in my chest. It reminds me of the feeling I get when I spend an entire Sunday building an incredible fort out of pillows, blankets, tables, chairs, garbage bags, and cereal boxes and then my mom tells me I have to clean it up before I go to bed even though I haven't gotten a chance to hang out inside of it because it took the entire day just to build it. And then before I can carefully take it apart Ruby runs in and demolishes the entire thing and my mom says I shouldn't be mad because I had to put it all away anyway and Ruby just helped me get it done quicker.

Not that that actually happened. Really.

After the barber finishes running the clippers over the sides of my head, he takes a pair of scissors and starts snipping the hair on top. Each time he takes one section between his fingers and cuts, I think he's done with that part, but then he grabs the same section again and cuts it even shorter. Suddenly there is a pile of orange hair swirls in my lap and on the floor all around my chair. The hair on my head is super short with spiky bits just above my forehead. I stare at myself in the mirror. I don't recognize the boy I see there at all. It's like a stranger staring back at me. But he definitely looks like a boy. And there is something slightly familiar about his look. I just can't figure out exactly what it is.

"I never thought I'd see the day when you got a buzz cut." Dad rubs his hand over the top of my head.

"Lemme try!" Ruby runs her hand over my head, too. "Oooh, soft. It's like unicorn fur."

"No, it's not!" I snap. "Unicorns have nothing to do with my hair."

"Louie." Dad frowns at me.

"I think it's very distinguished." Grandpa smiles at me in the mirror while my dad goes to pay. I look tough, like an army guy. It reminds me of someone.

The whole ride home I keep my hand hovering against the hair at the back of my head. The hair there is stiff, but also smooth, like really strong short grass. I can't remember ever lifting my hand to my head and feeling anything other than curls. It's like I'm touching somebody else's head. My forehead and neck are cold. I can sense the air against my skin there, where usually it is kept warm by hair. Maybe that's why a lot of boys wear baseball caps and other hats. Their heads are cold without much hair. Maybe I will start wearing a hat now.

When we get home and go into the kitchen, my mother and grandmother both make a fuss. It makes Princess run around in circles, the pink ribbons on her ears streaming down her back as she runs.

"You look so handsome!" My grandmother fans herself with an oven mitt. "All the girls in your grade will be smitten."

I make a face. Disgusting. I don't want anyone to be smitten.

"Your curls!" My mother makes a sad face. "I've never seen your face without them." She puts her hands on my cheeks.

"This is a much better haircut for a boy his age," my grandmother says.

And a much better haircut for a boy who wants people to know he's a boy.

"Why'd you cut it anyway? You don't look like you," says Ari. Her face looks different. More colorful. "Do you like it that way now?"

I look at my reflection in the glossy black surface of the oven door. I'm not sure if I like it yet. A part of me does and a part of me doesn't. "I wanted a change," I tell her. "You look different, too."

"Grandma did my makeup."

I look at Mom. Ari keeps asking if she can wear makeup but my mom always says no. She says Ari doesn't need makeup.

"It's just for Thanksgiving dinner," Ari explains.

"A girl deserves to dress up and have fun every now and then." Grandma puts her arms around my mom for a moment, then she goes to the oven and checks the turkey.

"Girls can have fun without makeup," my mom mumbles to herself. "That's just my opinion."

I don't know what's going on in my family, but it suddenly feels like everyone got turned upside down and twisted inside out. Ari and I look like different people. Grandma is letting Ari wear makeup, and Mom is letting Grandma be in charge. My dad is going away for two weeks even though he's *never* left before.

"Grandma, can we give my unicorns manicures and hornicures and lipstick cures? They aren't feeling well." Ruby holds up a green unicorn and makes a sad face. I guess she's the only one in my family who hasn't changed. She was strange enough already.

"Of course, sweetheart. We'll give them the whole spa treatment. We can give Princess a new outfit, too. I bought her a pilgrim costume."

Grandma and Princess play with Ruby, while Mom and Dad finish getting Thanksgiving dinner ready and Grandpa watches a football game and Ari takes pictures of herself on her phone. I go out to my comedy studio. I have to test something. I want to make sure I can be funny with short hair.

I bound onto my stage and grab the microphone. "Hello, garrrrage!" I pretend the garage is hooting and hollering.

"It's great to be here. You know what the difference between boys and girls is?"

I pause so the garage can think about this for a minute, then I tell it the answer.

"Neither does Thermos's uncle. You know what he called me today? A girl. That guy has serious problems. Boys and girls are total opposites. If he can't tell the difference between a boy and a girl, who knows what else he mixes up. He probably puts his dishes in the washing machine and his laundry in the dishwasher. Maybe he wears socks on his hands and mittens on his feet. And I'll bet he eats his napkin and wipes his mouth with spaghetti."

I switch the microphone to my other hand and sit down on my stool. "Really though, the main difference between boys and girls comes down to one thing. Boys are normal and girls are kooky. Boys laugh when something is funny. Girls giggle at strange and random times. Boys play during recess, girls stand around or sit on the swings. Boys are afraid of genuinely scary things like axe murderers and vampires. Girls are afraid of spiders and fuzz."

After I've got that off my chest I feel a little bit better. I mean, if you look at the examples, I'm clearly a boy. Uncle Joe is probably half blind and forgot to wear his glasses. I turn out the lights and head back inside, rubbing my new hair as I go. No one will make that mistake again.

LOVE, HEALTH, AND FOOTBALL

Thanksgiving is one of my favorite holidays. Here's why: sweet potatoes with Marshmallow Fluff. As much as I want. Grandma makes them, and they are part of the actual dinner. Not dessert. That means after a full plate of sweet potatoes with Marshmallow Fluff, I also get to eat pumpkin pie with whipped cream, plus an extra blast of whipped cream. Barflicious!

After my third serving of sweet potatoes, my mom suggests we all take turns saying what we are thankful for.

"I'll go first." My mother wipes the corners of her mouth with her napkin. "I am thankful for my three wonderful children, who make every day interesting and sweet. I am thankful for my husband, who is a caring father and a courageous man for taking a risk and following his dream. I am thankful for my job, which I truly enjoy, and I am thankful for my parents, especially my mom, for helping watch the kids for the next two weeks."

Mom dabs at the corners of her eyes with her napkin. I think she might be crying, which is weird since none of that stuff seemed sad.

"Who wants to go next?" Mom asks.

Ruby shoots her hand up in the air. "Me. Me. Pick me."

Where does she think she is? School?

"Okay, Ruby. Tell us what you are thankful for." My mom's smile is huge. It's as if she already knows Ruby is going to say something wacky and adorable. In my opinion, she's only half right.

"I am thankful for hair because if I didn't have it I would be bald." Ruby looks at Grandpa, who rubs a hand over his bald spot.

"I am thankful for unicorns because if I didn't have them I wouldn't be magical."

I roll my eyes at Ari, but Ari seems to be trapped under the Ruby-spell today, too. She shakes her head at me.

"Mostest of all, I am thankful for my whole family and Louie because if I didn't have them I would have to go in another family that might smell different."

Grandma looks shocked. Grandpa looks like he's trying to keep a straight face. It's classic Ruby. I hide my chuckle in my napkin.

"Okay, Ruby. Lovely," my mom says. "Who else would like to go?"

My grandma goes next, and she is thankful for us, for sunshiny days, and for Princess. Grandpa is thankful for love, health, and football. He pretends to throw me a pass. I don't react fast enough, so I fumble. Even at invisible football, I'm hopeless.

Ari goes next. "I am thankful that I still have my own room even though I have to let Grandma use it for the next two weeks, and I am thankful for my friends."

"Is that all?" my dad asks. He looks around the table. "Isn't there anything else?"

"Oh!" Ari nods. "I am thankful for all my new makeup! Thanks, Grandma!"

Dad puts his hand to his forehead, and I notice my mother give Grandma a "look." I'm not exactly sure what the look means, but it definitely means something. Probably that Mom is not as thankful about the makeup as Ari is.

"*I* am *very* thankful for my understanding family," my father says. "Thanks for letting me leave for two weeks. I am thankful for the generous donor who helped the library hire me, and to the other artist who had to cancel last minute so that the library hired me instead. I am thankful for all the people in the world who like to find beauty in strange things. I am thankful for my wife, who believes in me."

Dad leans over and gives Mom a big kiss.

I avert my eyes. Barfgusting. Some things are better kept private.

Everyone at the table turns to me; they all want to hear what I am thankful for, but I hate doing these kinds of things. I don't want to get all mushy and gushy and upchuck my feelings onto the table for everyone to dissect.

"I am thankful that it seems to be time for dessert! Break out the pie." I move my hands in a *ba-dum-ching* motion.

"Nice try," Mom says. "No dessert until you give us a serious answer. Come on, now."

I sigh. I don't know what I'm thankful for. It's not like I go around thinking about it all the time.

"Uh, I'm thankful for comedians? People who make up stuff that makes me laugh?"

Dad nods at me.

"That's a good one," Grandpa says.

"Oh! I thought of another one. I'm thankful for Marshmallow Fluff, the world's most perfect food."

Mom groans, and I take another scoop of sweet potatoes and eat all the Fluff off the top.

"Anything else?" Grandma asks.

I think about it for a second, then I add, "Nope."

Mom sighs. "I think it's time for dessert now."

She serves us each a slice of pumpkin pie with whipped cream, then my dad passes around the canister, and Ari, Ruby, and I spray whipped cream right into our mouths.

Mmmm. I am thankful for whipped cream.

On Friday morning, I ask my dad if he wants to work on our video, but he can't. He's got to finish loading the car. So I settle down on the couch to watch the Lou Lafferman marathon. Ari is sleeping in, Grandma and Ruby are making a unicorn costume for Princess, and Mom is out for a jog.

Lou is just about to start an "animals acting like people" segment, when Grandpa walks in. He's wearing one of his trademark tracksuits and the stomach is pooched out in a funny way. Maybe he ate too much turkey last night.

"Want to watch Lou with me?"

"I've got a better idea." He switches off the TV. "This is one of the last nice days of the year," he says. "In another month there'll be snow on the ground, and you'll be on your butt watching TV all the time. You've got to play outside while you still can."

"But it's *vacation*. And Ari and Ruby don't have to. And my dad can't work on my video, so there's nothing to do."

Grandpa reaches into the stomach of his tracksuit and pulls out a football. "Let's go toss the pigskin, huh? Make your old gramps happy?"

Ugh. I wish making Grandpa happy didn't have to make me unhappy. I wrinkle up the side of my nose.

"Now, you know I love your mom and her sisters,

and they all know how to snap a ball, but I didn't have any sons, Louie. You're my only grandson, and I just want to play my favorite game with my favorite boy. Is that too much to ask?"

I slide off the couch, feeling like I need to go back to sleep for about a thousand hours. "Okay," I tell him. I don't want to at all, but I can't stop thinking of Uncle Joe.

We head outside and it is pretty nice. The sun is shining, and even though there are no leaves on the trees, the grass still looks green and everything smells fresh. I take a deep breath. Maybe it won't be so bad.

"We'll start with throwing." He takes my left arm and tilts it up and back so my elbow is near the top of my head and my hand is pointing straight behind me. Then he positions the football in my hand. "Now I want you to throw it, letting go of the ball at the highest point and following through all the way with your palm down."

Huh? I think football might be a foreign language.

I try to do what Grandpa says but instead of the ball sailing all the way across the backyard the way I imagine, it sails straight down into the lawn in front of my feet.

"Nice follow-through," Grandpa says. "Now we'll just work on the timing of your release."

Grandpa sets me up for another try. I look longingly into our house through the family room window. The couch looks soft and comfy. I throw the ball again. This time the ball goes into the ground about five feet in front of me.

"Progress!" Grandpa picks up the ball and sets me up again. I take another quick look at the couch and this time I see Ari settling in with her comforter and turning on the TV. As soon as I see her, a thought races through my head. A thought so strange I snap my head back to Grandpa and listen to his football instructions like they are the most interesting thing in the whole entire world.

Because I absolutely don't want to think about my thought.

But every time Grandpa makes me throw the ball again, and again, and again, the thought pops back into my brain.

My life would be way easier if I was a girl.

SEE YA LATER

After an hour of throwing around the old pigskin, Grandpa wants to give me more football tips
but I've had enough. *My* favorite football tip is this:
when Grandpa can't stop talking about football,
hide. I tell him I need a drink of water and then
I sneak out to the Laff Shack.

Instead of learning more about football, I've
decided to work on my viral video. By myself. I
don't want people to forget about me, so I've got to
keep the viral videos coming. I can't wait around
until I get an idea for the next one. And I can't wait
around for my dad either.

I sit down in the middle of my stage (which is in
my comedy club, which is in my garage, in case you

haven't been paying attention), since that's where I do my best thinking. I'm sure a video idea will come to me soon. I lean back on my hands and look at the empty folding chairs facing the stage. The idea will be here any minute now.

Probably.

Almost certainly.

It might help if I straighten the chairs. Currently on the comedy club side, I have one stage and seven folding chairs. I'd have two more seats if I was willing to use the chairs from Ruby's old kiddie table, but for one thing, they are tiny, and for a worse thing, they are covered in Rainbow Lolli-girl stickers. Ruby used to be into Rainbow Lolli-girl before she became obsessed with Magical Mystery Unicorns.

Rainbow Lolli-girl versus the Unicorns of Doom? Nah.

If I want this video to go viral, it's going to have to be way cooler than that. It's hopeless. There is no way I'll be able to do it without Dad.

"There you are!" Mom opens the side door of the garage and pokes her head in. "It's time to say good-bye to Dad and Grandpa. The car's all packed."

I grab my comedy notebook and pencil and sit down on the front edge of my stage. "I'm a little busy," I tell her. "With Dad gone, I have to plan this whole video myself."

Mom tilts her head at me and gives me a sad smile. Then she comes and sits next to me on the stage so our shoulders are touching. "I'm going to miss Dad, too."

I tap my notebook with the eraser. "I'm not going to miss him," I tell her. "I just have a lot of stuff to do."

"Okay, you won't miss him." Mom leans in and gives me a shoulder-bump. "But you should still come say goodbye to him. And to Grandpa." Mom stands up and holds out her hand to me. "Come on."

I look at my notebook and sigh. "Okay."

At the end of the driveway, our old station wagon is loaded up with suitcases, art supplies, and junk.

Lots and lots of junk. Old license plates, broken bicycles, empty tin cans, and all kinds of stuff that people throw away.

Ruby is hugging Dad's leg so hard she's squeezing her eyes shut. Ari is talking to my dad, and I can't believe it, but she isn't even texting anyone while she talks to him. Maybe her phone is dead. Grandma and Grandpa stand behind them, watching. They have their arms around each other, and Grandma has Princess snuggled between them. She is wearing a sparkly unicorn horn. Princess. Not my grandmother. Grandma is wearing sparkly earrings.

"I found him," Mom calls as we walk down the driveway.

Dad takes a few steps toward me with his arms open for a hug. He has to walk like Frankenstein because Ruby won't let go of his leg.

I lean into him real quick, but step back before his arms close all the way around me. There is way too much hugging happening on our driveway today. Hugging is gross. Besides, I'm going to see

my dad again in less than two weeks, probably. I bet he finishes his art really early. I don't think hugs are necessary.

Ever since Dad first told me about the library job, I've been thinking about it. The pluses and the minuses. The pros and the cons. On the bad side, we'll miss two male-bonding times. With all the girls in our house, Dad and I need time to be guys together. Also on the bad side, without my dad, and with my grandma and Princess, the house girl-to-boy ratio becomes 5 to 1. That means my house will be approximately 84 percent female. I'm not certain, but it might be toxic for me to live in that kind of environment.

On the good side—well, I haven't figured out what the good side is yet, but I'm sure I will.

I look at Dad and imagine that I'm Tim Allen, the comedian who did the voice of Buzz Lightyear. His comedy routines are all about being a man. My chest puffs up and I put my hands on my hips. "Don't worry about a thing. I'll take care of everything while you're gone." I make my voice sound deep and grown-up, and my parents smile at each other.

Dad pries Ruby off his leg and lifts her up for a regular hug. "I'll miss you guys. Promise to call and do that computer-chat thingy, too."

Mom takes Ruby from my dad and kisses his cheek. "You should get going. You have to take Grandpa to the airport and then you've got a long drive after that. Make sure you take lots of rest breaks."

Grandpa climbs into the passenger seat and Dad sits behind the wheel.

"Bye, Daddy." Ari pulls her phone out and starts texting. "See you soon."

Dad turns on the engine.

"Hey, Dad," I call. "A photon walks into a hotel. The bellhop says, 'Can I help you with your bags?' 'No thanks,' says the photon. 'I'm traveling light.'"

Dad laughs. "Good one."

Ruby tugs the edge of my T-shirt. "I get it. Because a bellhop is a frog, right? Hop, hop, hop."

I shake my head. Ruby tries, but she's comically challenged. "The joke part is the photon. A photon is a tiny particle of light. So it's light that's traveling, but also it has no bags, so it's traveling light."

"Ooooh!" Ruby nods her head dramatically like she understands what I said, but I have my doubts.

Dad backs the car out of the driveway and then slowly drives up the street. He and Grandpa wave the entire way until he makes a left turn and the car disappears. I wipe my nose on my sleeve and clear my throat because it's a little scratchy. Probably because it's cold out. A chilly wind blows across the back of my naked neck. I have to remember to get a hat. The wind blows again and my nose drips and my eyes prickle, but it's not because I want to cry. I'm probably allergic to standing next to so many girls. Or I might be getting a cold. My nose isn't running because I want to cry. There is no reason to want to cry because I am not going to miss my dad. I'll probably barely even notice that he's gone.

WHAT GUYS DO

On Sunday, Nick and Thermos come over to hang out. Even though it's the last day of Thanksgiving Break, it's the first time I've seen them since the Turkey Bowl. On Friday and Saturday, Grandma made us go shopping and watch musicals and rent movies and bake our own pizzas.

"Whoa," says Nick when he sees me. "You got a haircut."

"I got *all* my hairs cut," I joke as we walk into the Laff Shack. We take off our jackets and leave them on my folding chairs.

"You look like Ryan Rakefield." Thermos smushes up her lips. "Like an orange-haired Ryan Rakefield."

"I do not," I say, but then I realize why this hairstyle seemed familiar. "Well, maybe we have the same hair spikes, but we don't have anything else in common."

"You're both boys," Thermos says.

We sit down on my stage and I shake my head. "I guess, but sometimes it feels like we are different species. I'm not even sure if Ryan is human. I mean, *you* have more in common with him than I do."

"No way," Thermos says. "Just because I like sports? I'm a good sport and he's a bad sport. That's not something we have in common. That's something we have in opposite."

"Well, how about Nick then? Maybe he's the most like Ryan."

"Me?" Nick points his thumb at his chest and widens his eyes in surprise.

Thermos and I look at each other and shake our heads. Then we crack up. Nick screws up his face like he doesn't get it, and that just makes Thermos and me laugh more. Sometimes it's like our brains are the same.

I put my feet up on the folding chair across from me. "What should we do? Board game?"

Thermos gives a half shrug. "Did you and your dad make a video? You could show it to us."

I point to Dad's side of the garage. "He had to leave for a job. I might not make a video anymore."

"What about your viral video plan? Your fans are waiting."

"I changed my mind," I say, even though my dad is really the one who changed it.

Thermos stares at me for a long time. I don't think she believes me.

"Let's just play soccer," Nick says.

"How about Zombie soccer?" I suggest.

Thermos tilts her head. "Why don't you make a video of us playing Zombie soccer?" she finally says.

"Fine." I know it won't be as good as if my dad helped me, but I definitely don't want to get into an argument with Thermos.

We put our jackets back on, Thermos finds a soccer ball, I grab our old video camera, and we start walking to the backyard. When we get to the lawn I realize Nick hasn't followed us.

"Hello? Earth to Nick. Zombie soccer movie?"

Nick hangs back, leaning into the door frame. "I have to tell you guys something." He shoves his hands in his pockets and looks at the ground. "But you might think it's weird."

"No, we won't," Thermos says. "Whatever it is, we won't care."

I'm not sure that's exactly true. I mean, we'd care if he told us he was moving to the city of Machu Picchu or if he told us that one of his knees had turned green. But I nod at him so he'll spill the beans.

"I'm going to ask Ava to Go Out," he tells us.

Thermos makes a face that I'd describe as politely disgusted. "Cool," she says, but she doesn't sound like she means it.

"Go out where?" I ask. "To the movies?"

He shakes his head.

"Bowling?"

Why would he want to go out with Ava? He can barely even talk when he's with her.

Nick scratches his head, then joins me and Thermos outside. We walk to the middle of my backyard. "I don't actually want to go anywhere with her. That would be weird. I just want to *Go Out* with her."

"Do you mean go outside? And stand there?" I turn on the video camera and point it at Nick. "Is this something you would do together, or are you just asking Ava to go outside by herself, because *that* would make sense."

Thermos laughs and punches me in the arm.

"Good one," she says. "But seriously, Nick, you should ask her to Go Out if you want to. I'm sure she'll say yes."

Nick exhales a big breath of relief. "Do you really think so? Maybe you could ask Hannah to ask Ava what she would say."

I turn off the video camera and hang my head. "You sound like Ari and all her crazy friends. Why do you have to ask somebody to ask somebody to ask somebody?"

"You don't understand," Nick says. "It's what guys do."

I'm a guy, I want to tell him, and it's not what I do. But I don't. This whole conversation makes my shoulders feel like they are squeezing in. Nick's body might have been invaded by an alien. I can't think about it anymore. "Let's start with some shots of both of you emerging from the ground like the undead."

I set up my camera on a tripod. Then we rake whatever leaves we can find on the ground. Most of the leaves have already been cleared from the yard, but we find enough to make two piles, and those will be the graves Nick and Thermos rise out of at the beginning of the Zombie soccer match.

I form a pile at each side of my yard with the soccer ball in the middle. Nick and Thermos lurch out of their piles, arms outstretched, jaws hanging open. Then, once they are standing, they both pretend to notice the soccer ball. They race, super-slow-Zombie style, to reach the ball. I make sure the camera cuts back and forth between them. Thermos gets to the ball first, but instead of kicking it she does a great improvisation. She picks the ball up and pretends to eat it. Nick shuffles around Thermos like he really wants a bite, too.

"Cut!" I shout after a couple of minutes. I play it back for Nick and Thermos.

"It's great," Thermos says. "You should post it. Maybe it will go viral."

"Nah," I say. It's not bad, but it's no mustache omelet.

"Maybe one day we could make a video with Ava," Nick suggests.

"Why?" I ask.

"Nick wants to be in a romance movie," Thermos says.

"Eww," I say, as Nick says, "Not a *romance*, just a video." But somehow I get the feeling a romance doesn't sound that bad to him. And that's just weird. I look at Thermos and pretend to barf. She crosses her eyes. At least I have one friend who will never change.

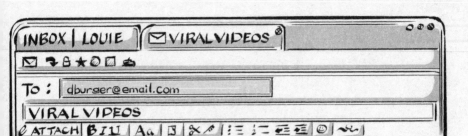

INBOX | LOUIE | ✉ VIRALVIDEOS ®

To : dburger@email.com

VIRAL VIDEOS

ATTACH B I U | Aa | ✂ | | | | | | ☺ | ✎

Hi, Dad.
    I know you are busy, but I wondered if there is any way you can help me make a video while you are out of town. I made a Zombie video today, but it's not the same without you.
    Also, Nick is going to ask a girl to **Go Out**.
Your son,
Louie

THE PROBLEM WITH GRANDMAS

When I wake up Monday morning, at first I think it's a regular morning, and that I'm going to walk into the kitchen and find my dad holding up two boxes of cereal. "Lucky Charms or Cap'n Crunch," he'll say. "Breakfast can be a big decision."

But when I hear the high-pitched voice trailing down the hallway to my bedroom, I'm instantly jolted back to the present moment. *"Chain, chain, chain!"*

It's Grandma, singing her old-lady songs at top volume. Now I remember. Dad's out of town, Mom's at work, and Grandma is in charge.

"Aroof, arooof!" Princess is singing, too.

I pull my pillow over my head because it's bad

enough being woken up by a singing grandma, but it's worse being woken up by your singing grandma and your singing grandma's singing dog.

"Morning, Grandma!" I hear Ari shout from her bedroom.

I pull my covers over my pillow. My grandma is the loudest waker-upper in the entire world.

"Princess!" Ruby's excitement is so loud even my pillow and comforter don't muffle it.

"Arf, arf, arfarfarfarfarf."

"We are going to have so much fun these next two weeks. Spa and craft nights, shopping and more shopping, and I've got some great new recipes to teach you."

I hear feet shuffling across the hallway to my room and I try to make myself invisible, even though I know that's impossible. I don't know how I am going to make it through the next two weeks.

It's not that I don't love my grandma, because I do. I love her a lot. I just don't *like* her all the time. First, she does the usual annoying grandma things like pinch my cheeks and leave lipstick on my forehead every time she sees me. But she also sings constantly, even in public, and she dresses Princess in sparkly pink dog clothes. And she's always reminding me how cute I was when I was three and spent one whole vacation trying to walk in her high-heeled shoes.

Um. That didn't actually happen. Really.

I guess what I'm trying to say is that if my mom and Ari and Ruby are girls, then Grandma is a triple girl, no, a quadruple girl. She always looks fancy, even when she's in her silky pajamas.

Princess is even worse. The girliest dog you could ever imagine. She doesn't play fetch. She doesn't roll around on the floor and wrestle, but she'll sit still for forty-three minutes while Ari and Ruby dress her up like a unicorn.

"Rise and shine, Louie Lou!" Grandma pulls my covers back, plucks the pillow away from my face, and plants a huge lipsticky kiss right above my left eye. "Wake up, handsome prince, I've made a special breakfast for you!"

And before I can say yuck and wipe the lipstick

away, Grandma sprinkles glitter all over my bed. "It's magic wake-up dust!"

Grandma dances out of my room, singing, *"You better think (think) think about what you're trying to do to me."*

I roll out of bed and into the bathroom, and

A diagram of Grandma, who is a girl

[1a.] Sings all the time, even in public

[1b.] Lipstick she leaves on my forehead

[1c.] fancy pjs

[2a.] pink sparkly dog clothes

⟨ fig 2. Princess, her dog

⟨ fig 1. Grandma

because of Grandma's kiss I actually have to wash my face with soap instead of splashing water on my skin and pretending that I washed my face. Even with the soap, I can't get all the lipstick off, so I'll have to go to school with the faint impression of red lips on my forehead. Maybe I should wear my old tennis headband.

When I get to the kitchen, Grandma is standing in front of the stove scrambling eggs. She is wearing a purple-and-white-polka-dot apron with black ruffles. She has set a plate of pink flower-shaped pancakes in the center of the table. Each plate has a napkin in a fancy company napkin ring. Next to the plates, orange juice is served in wineglasses. She is also talking on her cell phone.

"That is unacceptable. The mascara shipment was supposed to be in yesterday. If it's not there by ten this morning, you will have to eat my costs."

I pull out a chair and Grandma smiles at me over her shoulder when she hears it scrape across the floor. "I've got to go," she says to the person on the other end. "I'll call you at ten."

"Um, Grandma," I say when she's put her phone in her apron pocket. "I usually just make myself a bowl of cereal." I do not want to eat pink-flower pancakes. I sit down at the table, but I don't serve myself. I'm not even sure if I'm supposed to. It feels like I'm in a fancy restaurant instead of my own kitchen.

Grandma steps over to me and scoops some eggs onto my plate. Then she gives me a pancake and a slice of honeydew melon. "Well, then, today you'll finally get a real breakfast."

I don't know what she means. Cereal is a real breakfast. It's the breakfast of champions. I eat the eggs and the melon and sneak my pancake to Princess.

Ari walks into the kitchen with Ruby bouncing along behind her. "This looks great, Grandma!" Ari gives her a hug. "Dad usually makes us get our own breakfast."

Grandma shakes her head and puts eggs on Ari's and Ruby's plates. "You won't have to do *that* this week. You all need some *grandmothering*!"

"I like cereal," I say with my mouth full of eggs. "Dad is teaching us independence."

Grandma kisses my forehead and singsongs, "Mind your p's and q's."

"I like cereal and pancakes and syrup and eggs and oatmeal and waffles and honeymoo melon." Ruby pours syrup over all the food on her plate and takes a big bite.

"As soon as you are finished eating breakfast, please brush your teeth and gather your things. I want to leave extra time to drive you to school this morning since I'm new to the route."

I swallow down a bite of eggs. "Ruby and I don't need a ride. We walk."

Grandma takes off her apron and tucks it through the handle of the oven door. "I'm going to be driving Ari, so I might as well drive everyone. Otherwise I'd have to leave you and Ruby home alone while I'm gone with your sister. No arguments! Now, I'm going to finish getting ready and we'll leave in ten minutes."

Grandma struts out of the kitchen singing about feeling like a natural woman, whatever that is.

When she's out of earshot, I whisper to Ari and Ruby, "What are we going to do?"

"About what?" Ari slices her melon into a bunch of neat pieces and takes a bite.

"About Grandma!" I gesture toward the hallway, and Princess runs off in that direction barking. I guess she's wondering what I'm pointing to. "How are we going to take ten days of singing and lipstick kisses and *grandmothering*?"

"I like it." Ruby piles her eggs between two syrupy pancakes, then picks the whole thing up and eats it like a sandwich. "Grandma said we could go shopping and she will get me a new unicorn to go with the mountain hideout Daddy's going to make me."

Ari pushes out her bottom lip and thinks about it for a second. She squints one eye like she's thinking about it another way. Then she takes a bite of pancakes. "Sorry. Can't help you. I like having Grandma here. She's going to do my colors, get me more makeup, and give me a make-over."

I sigh. *This* is the problem with having sisters instead of brothers. I'm totally outnumbered.

TOP TEN WORST
WAYS TO GET WOKEN UP

1. BY AN ANIMAL LICKING YOUR FACE... WHEN YOU **DON'T** HAVE A PET.
2. BY YOUR YOUNGER SISTER LICKING YOUR FACE. (**DON'T ASK!**)
3. BY YOUR OLDER SISTER HITTING YOU IN THE FACE WITH A PILLOW.
4. BY **BOTH** OF YOUR SISTERS JUMPING ON YOUR BED, **AND** YOUR LEGS, **AND** YOUR STOMACH, **AND** YOUR HEAD.
5. BY A DREAM THAT YOU HAVE TO GO TO THE BATHROOM REALLY, **REALLY** BAD. BUT EVERY TIME YOU WALK INTO A BATHROOM IT TURNS INTO THE LAUNDRY ROOM UNTIL FINALLY YOU FIND A BATHROOM AND YOU GO AND THEN YOU WAKE UP AND REALIZE YOU WENT. UM... THAT DIDN'T **ACTUALLY** HAPPEN. **REALLY!**
6. BY A BOBBLEHEAD FALLING OFF YOUR SHELF AND LANDING RIGHT NEXT TO YOUR EYES SO THAT WHEN YOU OPEN THEM, STARTLED, YOU SEE BOZO THE CLOWN NODDING AT YOU.
7. BY YOUR DAD SAYING, "**WAKE UP! WE WON THE LOTTERY!**" AND THEN SAYING "CAN YOU BELIEVE IT? WE WON **FIVE DOLLARS!**"
8. BY YOUR MOM SAYING, "**WAKE UP!** WE ARE GOING TO DO A **TEN-MILE FAMILY RUN!**" AND THEN SAYING, "**APRIL FOOLS!** WE ARE ONLY GOING TO DO A **TWO-MILE RUN.**"
9. BY A STRANGE VOICE SAYING, "I LOVE YOU, BUNNYWUFFLEKINS," AND REALIZING IT IS YOUR OLD TALKING TEDDY THAT YOU USED TO SLEEP WITH BUT YOU HAVE NO IDEA HOW IT GOT IN YOUR BED WITH YOU.
10. BY A GRANDMA/DOG DUET.

N-O-!

While Grandma drives me and Ruby and Ari to school, I pretend Nick is in the car, too, so that I'm not the only boy. If I were walking to school, Nick and I would have played Backpack War and Spit (not the card game, but Spit with actual spit). I also pretend my dad is really driving the car because he would have laughed when I told him that turning my socks inside out was the same as putting on a new pair. But I'm not with Nick and I'm not with Dad. Grandma drove back home and made me change my socks. For the entire car ride, I have to listen to Grandma play Aretha Franklin on the stereo and plan makeovers and unicorn tea parties with my sisters.

Princess sits in the backseat between Ruby and me. I squish myself against the door of the car and think about Tim Allen so my mind doesn't get girl-melded. Tim Allen says in his comedy routine that all men like tools, so I imagine screwdrivers and wrenches and hammers dancing around the car. When he's being really manly and talking about tools, Tim Allen grunts.

"Unh, unh, unh!"

"Goodness, Louie! Are you all right?" Grandma peers into the backseat at me as Ari climbs out of the passenger seat for school. I notice she's wearing sparkly stuff on her eyes. Princess barks and jumps into Ruby's lap.

Um, did I grunt out loud?

"I'm fine," I tell her. "Just clearing my throat." Clearing out all the girliness.

Grandma *tsk*s and reaches her hand back to feel my forehead. "I hope you aren't coming down with something."

I am. It's called girl-itis.

I shake my head. "I'm fine."

"Louie just likes to make noises," Ruby explains as Grandma pulls away from Ari's school and drives us to Barker.

When we get to school, I cannot wait to find Nick and Thermos. They are the only two people in the world who will be able to understand what I'm going through. It's Attack of the Girlzillas at my house. I don't know how I'm going to survive being the only boy for ten more days.

Grandma drops us off in the car-pool line, and Ruby races over to her first-grade friends, barking like Princess. Maybe she'll be into dogs now instead of unicorns.

I trudge past the second-, third-, and fourth-grade sections of the blacktop to the area where the fifth graders line up for school. Grandma's crazy song about feeling like a natural woman is stuck in my head even though I don't want to feel like a natural woman. I want to feel normal. I want to feel funny. I want to feel barftastic. I'd even settle for feeling weird.

I find Thermos and Nick over on the basketball

court. They are playing N-O-! It's just like H-O-R-S-E, but faster because you're out after two letters and one punctuation mark.

Ava and her friend Hannah are watching. And whispering. And giggling. Typical girls! I'd like to ask them both to Go Out right now. Out of my personal space, that is.

Thermos tosses me the ball. "Nick has N-O and I have nothing. The shot is standing on one foot from the wood chip shaped like a nose."

I leave my backpack by the edge of the court, catch the ball, and stand on the wood chip shaped like a nose. I lift my left foot, toss the ball, and catch the right rim. The ball circles twice, then falls in. "Yes!" I punch my hand in the air and pass the ball to Nick.

"Where were you this morning?" he asks.

"My grandma drove me to school." I stand near Thermos so I'm not in Nick's way. He stands on his left foot, wobbles back and forth, and shoots without looking at the basket.

"In her pink car?"

My grandma owns a pink Cadillac, to be specific. And every time she goes for a drive she starts by singing a song about a pink Cadillac driving on a freeway of love. Blech. That's a real song. She's played it for me about a million times.

Nick's ball clanks the front edge of the rim and rebounds right. Thermos dives for it and Nick calls out, "That's N-O-!"

It might be my imagination, but he doesn't seem too broken up about getting out. He actually seems happy. He skip-runs over to Ava while Thermos sets up her next shot.

"Kneecap layup." She gets on her knees just to the side of the basket and does a perfect layup.

Layups aren't exactly my best shot. Usually *I'm* the first person to get out, but there is no way I'm going to stand with the girls today. I may not love sports, but they are better than unicorns and makeup and . . . Wait!

Ava just gave Nick a bracelet. It's black and green and looks like it's made out of rubber bands. He's putting it on. A bracelet. I can't think why he would wear a bracelet. He probably doesn't want to hurt her feelings by refusing it.

This is serious! I cannot get out. I do not want to stand with the girls and wear a bracelet. I look hard at the basket and concentrate with all my might. I arc the ball exactly like Thermos taught me. *Swish.*

That's what I'm talking about. We keep playing until the bell rings, and I make every shot, although my brain aches from concentrating so hard. Then we head inside for school.

After attendance, social studies, and fifteen minutes of silent reading, it's time to go to music. I don't mind music too much. It's better than gym. At least I can carry a tune. If only we picked teams in music instead of gym, maybe I'd see what it was like to be picked first.

Mrs. Lineball, the music teacher, claps out a rhythm as my class arrives. She likes us to walk to the rhythm until we take our seats. I step, step-step, step, step-step, then I sit down between Nick and Jamal. Thermos sits on Jamal's other side, and Ava sits next to Nick. We tap our feet to the beat until Mrs. Lineball lifts one hand up, fingers wide open, and quickly makes a fist. When we see the fist, we go silent.

"Thank you," says Mrs. Lineball, sorting through a messy pile of papers on top of her piano while she talks. "Today we are going to start working on the Fifth-Grade Sing. I've chosen a really special program for us to do. It's called *Free to Be . . . You and Me*. We will sing some of the songs together, and then I will assign duets and solos for the other stories, songs, and skits. I think you will really like it!"

Mrs. Lineball looks through a different pile of papers on her desk and finds a CD buried at the bottom. She plays a recording of a song for us. It's kind of weird. It's about a land where children and rivers and horses are free and then they grow up. It's got a lot of flowery language, but I guess it sounds pretty nice. Mrs. Lineball has us read the words rhythmically a couple of times (she's really into rhythm), then she teaches us the first verse. When class is almost over, we stop singing. Mrs. Lineball stands up and leans her elbow on the top of the piano. A couple pieces of sheet music fall off the edge.

"If I call your name, please come see me over here. The rest of you may line up at the door. Theodora Albertson, Ryan Rakefield, Ava Gonzales, Louie Burger, Owen Gleiberman."

I look at Thermos with my eyes wide and pull the side of my bottom lip down like I'm scared we are in trouble. But Mrs. Lineball is smiling at us, so I'm pretty sure that's not why she called our names. She hands each of us a sheet of paper and a CD in a paper sleeve.

"I'd like each of you to have a special part in the show. Some of you will sing and some will have a speaking part. Please listen to these CDs and review your stories or songs tonight."

Ryan scowls and folds his arms across his chest. "I don't want to sing alone. It's weird."

Mrs. Lineball takes a deep breath. She looks like she's really annoyed, but trying to hold it in. Grownups always think they can hide when they are annoyed with kids, but they can't. It's kind of funny as long as I'm not the one who's causing the annoyance.

"Don't worry. I've given you a speaking part, Ryan. I will be contacting your parents about scheduling three or four extra rehearsals before or after school for the students with featured roles."

"I don't think my mom can drive me," Ryan says. "She works, and so does my dad. I take the bus."

Mrs. Lineball nods, then tilts her head like she's thinking about what Ryan said. "Well, maybe I can help set up a car pool or something. Or maybe I can pull you out during class. I'm sure your parents will be excited to see you perform. We'll be able to work something out."

"Are you ready for me?" Mrs. Adler stands in the doorway at the head of the line.

"Oh, goodness. I hope I didn't keep you waiting." Mrs. Lineball shoos us toward the line, tripping over a pile of rhythm sticks left on the floor. "Oops! We're finished."

As we walk back to class, I glance down at the sheet of paper Mrs. Lineball gave me. The words at the top of the paper say "William's Doll."

I fold my paper in half as quickly as I can so no

one will see what it says. Mrs. Lineball wants me to sing a song about a boy with a doll?

I think the expression that applies here is: When pigs fly.

INBOX | LOUIE | ✉ MISS YOU ⊗

✉ ⤵ ⊟ ★ ⊘ ▢ 🖨

To : | burgerboy@email.com
FROM | dburger@email.com
SUBJECT: | MISS YOU
🖇 ATTACH | B I U | Aa | 🖹 | ✂ ✏ | ⁝☰ ⁚☰ ☲ ☲ | ☺ | ⌇ | 6:00am

Sorry I didn't e-mail you back yesterday. I got in really late and I was pooped! I'm going to be setting up all day today, and then going out to dinner with the library board tonight. Fancy restaurant and free food. My favorite kind of dinner.
I don't think we can work on your video until I get home. I'll be too busy. But keep thinking of ideas!
So Nick wants a girlfriend. That's different, huh? Is it Thermos?
We'll do a computer chat tomorrow, okay?
And I'll keep thinking about videos, too.

MORE DISGUSTING THAN STEPPING IN SNOT

The next day at lunch, Nick asks Thermos if Thermos has asked Hannah if Hannah will ask Ava what Ava would say if Nick asked her to Go Out. At least, I think that's what he asked Thermos. The whole thing is way too barfomplicated. Thinking about it hurts my head. Besides, I can't stop worrying about the fifth-grade music show. There is no way I can do my part. Mrs. Lineball pulled Thermos and Ryan out of class this morning for their first rehearsal. I have a feeling I'm next unless I think of something fast.

"I'll ask her," Thermos says to Nick. "I promise. But it's not like I talk to Hannah all the time or anything. I can't just go up to her in the middle of the day. Maybe when we are on the bus."

Nick looks at Ava like he's not sure he can wait that long. "Okay," he says, sighing.

"You've got to be casual," Jamal tells Nick. "Be patient."

"Or . . . you could just ask Ava to Go Out right now, if you can't wait," I say.

Nick looks at me like I'm crazy. "That's not how it works."

Jamal shakes his head at me. "Definitely not how it works."

If you ask me, how it works is what's crazy.

Thermos slurps up a noodle from her chicken noodle soup, then looks at me and says, "What part did you get in the show? I'm reading a story about a girl who's really good at baseball, but her friend won't let her play on the boys' team. I have to read it with Ryan." She makes a face.

"Oh." I tilt my head back and look up at the ceiling like I'm thinking really, really hard. Thermos's and Ryan's parts seem perfect for them. Mrs. Lineball obviously chose them because they fit their parts in real life. Is that why she chose me? If I tell Thermos what my song is called, will she think I play with dolls?

I look at Thermos and shake my head. "I can't remember my part. Anyway, I'm not sure I can do it. I have stage fright, you know."

Thermos gives me a funny look. "Your stage fright isn't that bad anymore. And you like to perform. Why don't you really want to be in the fifth-grade show?"

"I do want to be in the show. I just . . . Singing alone is weird."

"You sang 'The Burp Song' alone in the talent show," Nick says.

"That didn't exactly go well for me. I threw up in front of millions of people."

Sheesh. Suddenly it feels like everyone is ganging up on me. But they are wrong. Singing alone *is* weird if you have to sing about a boy who wants to play with a doll. Mrs. Lineball could have picked any boy in fifth grade. Does she think that I actually like playing with dolls?

"Singing for comedy is different from singing for real. I'm going to ask Mrs. Lineball to give my part to someone else."

"No way," says Jamal. "It's cool to have a solo. You should do it."

Thermos raises an eyebrow at me. "I think that haircut has affected your brain. You're starting to sound like Ryan Rakefield."

I shrug and take a bite of my sandwich. Yuck. I forgot Grandma packed my lunch today. I was expecting a sweet, peanut butter-y bite of Fluffernutter and instead I got tuna salad. I wrap the sandwich back up in foil and dump the rest of the contents of my lunch box in front of me, hoping Grandma packed something edible. Along with an apple, a yogurt tube, some carrot sticks, and a Baggie of graham crackers, a piece of red paper shaped like a heart flutters to the floor. I see Nick, Jamal, and Thermos looking at it, but I snatch it up before anyone else notices, hopefully.

I hold it under the table so I can figure out what the heck this heart is. It has writing on the back.

Hearts are red,
Blueberry yogurt is blue,
♡ ♥ I sure do love
♡ Packing lunches for you. ♡
Love, Grandma

I feel like I've been slimed with extra-syrupy girliness. Doesn't Grandma know that boys do not want heart love poems in their lunch?

"Hi, Nick."

I look up and Ava and Hannah are standing right next to me. Ava and Nick are staring at each other, but Hannah is trying to peek under the table. I quickly shove the poem at Jamal.

"What was that?" Hannah asks me.

"What was what?" I say, rearranging my food so I don't have to look up at her.

"That piece of paper." She points at Jamal's hand. "It looks like a heart. Are you Going Out with someone?" she asks him.

"This isn't mine!" Jamal shoves the heart back at me.

"Oh." Hannah smiles, then turns to me. "Are *you* Going Out with someone?"

Thermos snaps her head up and squints her eyes at me.

"No way! Going Out with someone is more disgusting than accidentally eating dog food. Or stepping in snot. Or watching somebody's skin get peeled off on the medical channel."

I make a disgusted face, but I don't think Hannah believes me. She's looking at my pocket in a way that says, *If I stare hard enough, I bet I'll get X-ray vision.* Then I notice Nick looking down at the table, kind of embarrassed and angry at the same time. Oops. I look at Ava. Her cheeks are turning pink. Jamal has his arms folded across his chest, and even Thermos has a funny look on her face.

Um, I think the expression that applies here is: I just put my foot in my mouth.

Jamal shakes his head at me.

"That's what some people say," I continue. "But not me. I think when two people want to Go Out, then it's not disgusting at all. It's like unicorns dancing in a field of rainbows."

I glance at Thermos and roll my eyes so at least one person will know I'm not serious. Thermos starts pressing her thumb into the crumbs on the table. I know she hates talking about this stuff as much as I do. Ava and Hannah giggle uncontrollably.

Finally Ava elbows Hannah and Hannah says, "Um, do you guys want to play H-O-R-S-E at recess?"

I say, "With you?" at the same time that Nick says, "Sure."

"I'll play," Jamal says.

Thermos looks back and forth at all of us. Then

she shrugs and says, "I'll play anything with anyone."

"We'll just watch," Ava says, "like before. Okay? See you outside." Hannah and Ava walk over to the trash cans to throw away their lunch garbage.

"Why would anyone want to spend their whole recess just watching someone else play?" I say.

Thermos shrugs.

"I might watch, too," says Nick. "I'm not in the mood for H-O-R-S-E."

That's strange. Nick is always in the mood for H-O-R-S-E. Nick, Thermos, Jamal, and I stand up and suddenly I have a terrible thought. What if being a girl is contagious, and when you decide to like a girl and ask her to Go Out it makes you start acting more and more like a girl? What if that's happening to Nick?

I will never, ever, ever like a girl.

WHAT'S THE DEAL WITH LUNCH BOX NOTES?

WHY DO MOMS AND GRANDMAS THINK THAT KIDS NEED A NOTE IN THEIR LUNCH BOX? IT MIGHT BE OKAY FOR A FIRST OR SECOND GRADER, BUT OLDER THAN THAT AND IT STARTS TO GET EMBARRASSING.

SERIOUSLY, AS LONG AS THERE IS FOOD IN MY LUNCH BOX I KNOW THAT YOU LOVE ME. YOU DON'T NEED TO PUT IT IN WRITING. PERHAPS IF YOU PACKED ME A **SEVERED HAND**, THEN I CAN SEE WHERE A NOTE WOULD BE APPROPRIATE. THAT'S THE KIND OF THING THAT REQUIRES AN EXPLANATION.

OR, IF YOU PACKED A **LIVE RODENT**, OR A **FLASH DRIVE** WITH **TOP-SECRET INFORMATION** THAT WILL MAKE ME A TARGET OF **INTERNATIONAL ASSASSINS**, THEN I CAN SEE WHERE I'D LIKE A LITTLE HEADS-UP.

BUT IF ALL YOU'RE GIVING ME IS A SANDWICH, CHIPS, AN APPLE, AND A COOKIE, THEN THAT'S PRETTY SELF-EXPLANATORY. **NO NOTES, PLEASE!**

THE EVEN BIGGER PROBLEM WITH GRANDMAS

When Ruby and I get home from school, our entire house smells like a bakery, warm and chocolaty and sugary.

"Hang up your things and come to the kitchen," Grandma calls to us as I close the door. "I made you a special treat."

We walk into the kitchen, and the table is set with place mats and tiny plates and teacups. In the center of the table sits a platter of fresh-baked chocolate chip cookies and a bowl of strawberries. I take a deep inhale. Now I know why the house smells so good.

Ari is already sitting there eating strawberries. Her face is even more sparkly than it was yesterday.

"Now," Grandma says as she sits next to Ruby and across from me and Ari, "I want to hear all about your days."

I put two cookies and a pile of strawberries on my plate.

"I got to be line leader today," Ruby says. Her voice is serious, like she's reporting a special news broadcast. "Stinky Kate got the Magical Mystery Unicorn Mountain Hideout and she brought Rainbow Thunder to school, but she wouldn't let me hold Rainbow Thunder or even pet her mane because I told her Daddy was going to build me my own Magical Mystery Unicorn mountain with a waterfall and she said that would be a fake mountain and I said it would not and she said I was a liar and I said she was a bidiot."

Ari and I sneak looks at each other and smirk, but Grandma puts her hand on Ruby's hand and says, "I'm sorry your friend called you a liar. That wasn't very nice of her, but you can't call people idiots. That's not nice either."

"She's not my friend." Ruby reaches for another

cookie and takes a bite. "She says I can't play with the girls because I only play with Henry and I have boy germs."

"*What?*" Grandma sits back and her eyes go wide with shock. "Do your parents know what this girl says to you?"

Ruby nods as she gulps milk from her teacup. "Uh-huh. Daddy says Stinky Kate has mean germs and it's a good thing I like playing with Henry better anyway."

Grandma makes a *tsk*ing sound, then purses her lips. I think Dad's advice sounds good, but Grandma doesn't look as if she thinks so. "Wouldn't it be nice if you could play with all the children in your class?"

"Henry is probably way more fun than a bunch of stinky girls." I hold my teacup out to Ruby so we can clink.

Ruby toasts with me. "Henry is my bestest friend because he is my only friend."

Grandma *tsk*s again.

"Well, I had a terrible day if anyone wants to know," Ari announces.

"Eh. I'll pass," I say. But I wag my eyebrows at Ari so she'll know I'm kidding. Sort of.

"What happened, sweetheart?" Grandma gives Ari another cookie.

"Can you tell Mom that everyone in my grade wears eye shadow to school. I'm the *only* person who doesn't."

"I don't see the harm in a little lip gloss," Grandma says. "Maybe she'll see reason if I teach you how to apply it the right way for a tweenager."

I laugh. "A tweenager? That's not a real thing."

"That's what the ladies at Flashy Face Cosmetics

call our youngest customers." Grandma smiles and smooths her apron. "I'm sure I can convince her."

"Thank you, thank you!" Ari picks up her phone and starts texting. "You're the best, Grandma!"

"Anything for my granddaughters," Grandma says. "And how about you, Louie? Did anything interesting happen to you today?"

I think about Nick and Ava, but don't want to tell Grandma about that. "Nope. Nothing."

"Nothing at all?" Grandma asks. "Are you sure?"

Something about the way she asks makes me feel funny. As though she's expecting a certain answer rather than just asking out of curiosity.

"Well, I found a piece of gum in my coat pocket that I forgot about. It wasn't even chewed. That was sort of interesting."

"Maybe we have different definitions of interesting." Grandma purses her lips. "Your music teacher called today. You have a solo! I'm so proud. And don't worry, I will help you practice."

"You're singing a solo?" Ari bugs her eyes.

"Like 'The Burp Song'!" Ruby has arranged her

strawberries on her plate in the shape of a happy face. She starts singing the song I wrote for the fifth-grade talent show a couple of months ago. *"I drink a can of soda, and make a sound like Yoda . . ."*

"It's not like 'The Burp Song' and I'm not singing a solo. Mrs. Lineball asked me to, but that was yesterday and I'm not going to do it."

"Not going to do it?" Grandma looks shocked. "No. You *have* to. You are a wonderful singer."

"Yeah but the song is—" I'm about to tell them that the song is about a boy who wants to play with dolls, but before I do, I imagine their reactions in my head. Ruby will say that I play with unicorns, and Ari will say the song is definitely weird, and Grandma will tell me I am a wonderful singer again.

I don't want to describe the song out loud because more than what they will say, I know what they will wonder. They will wonder why Mrs. Lineball chose *me* to sing that song. My mind flashes for a second to Uncle Joe.

I don't want anyone to wonder anything about me. "I don't want to sing."

Grandma stands up and starts clearing the serving plates, food, and teacups from the table. I grab one last cookie before she whisks the platter away. As she stands at the counter wrapping the leftover cookies in foil, she looks at me and shakes her head. "That doesn't seem like a very good reason. Sometimes the things we don't want to do actually turn out to be pretty great. I seem to remember your mother telling me you didn't want to do the school talent show at first, and look how well that turned out. Maybe this will surprise you."

"I don't care," I say. "I still don't want to do it."

"Louie, now you are being unreasonable. You should at least give it a try before you say no. Try it for a week, and then you can decide."

I stare at the cookie on my plate. I wanted it a minute ago, but now I've lost my appetite. I thought grandmas were supposed to spoil their grandchildren and let them do (or *not* do) whatever they want. Grandma said yes to Ari and makeup. Why didn't she say yes to no singing?

I believe the expression that applies here is: *Et tu*, Grandma?

○ ○ ○

That night after dinner, my mom and my sisters and I gather around the computer to talk to my dad. Mom sits in the chair with Ruby in her lap. Ari and I stand right behind her shoulders. As Dad talks, his face keeps freezing so his words don't exactly line up with his lips all the time, but it still feels good to see his face, even if he hasn't been gone that long. I'm not missing him or anything, but I need to tell him about the song. If I can get Dad to say I don't have to do it, then Grandma can't make me wait a week to decide.

"How's it going?" Mom asks.

"Busy." Dad runs his fingers through his hair. "I don't know why, but it's taking twice as long to unpack as it did to pack. I spent all day Sunday setting up in the lobby of the library. They've got a space for me surrounded by a portable fence. There was one little boy and his babysitter who watched me for about two hours yesterday, and I wasn't even making anything yet, I was still unloading boxes. Then today, I worked in front of a crowd. I even signed a few autographs." Dad laughs. His face laughs three seconds later.

I'm about to tell Dad that Grandma's going to make me perform in the Fifth-Grade Sing, but Ari starts talking first.

"Grandma said she'd teach me how to do my makeup," Ari tells Dad. "She thinks it's fine for me to wear it to school."

"That sounds great, hon! Send me a picture."

"She did?" says my mom. "What about what your *mom* says?"

"Grandma said she'd talk to you later." Ari shrugs, and Mom takes a deep breath and closes her eyes.

"Speaking of Grandma," I say. "She wants me to—"

"I got to be line leader today!" Ruby leans forward

so she can put her face right up close to the computer camera.

"Hi, Ruby. Did you choose marching feet or tippy-toe?" Dad asks.

"Tippy marching, and Stinky Kate said there was no such thing as tippy marching, but then I showed her and she said tippy marching was dumb but Mr. Beauregard said we could still do tippy marching since I was the line leader and I got to pick."

"Of course there's such a thing as tippy marching!" Dad laughs. "I tippy march all the time."

"Dad, I got assigned a solo in the Fifth-Grade Sing and—"

"That's great, Louie! I'm so proud of you." Dad starts to smile, but his face freezes in the middle so the smile looks weird and lopsided.

"No! It's not good. It stinks. I don't want to sing it."

Dad gives me a sympathetic face and Mom reaches back and rubs my arm. "Why don't you want to do it?" he asks.

"Because it's about—" I start to tell him, but then I stop myself. If he was at home and we were in our man cave, or having male-bonding time, I could definitely tell my dad. He'd understand, and I know he wouldn't make me do it. But I can't tell him now, not with Mom, Ari, and Ruby all listening in. I don't want anyone to know Mrs. Lineball thinks I should sing about dolls. "I just don't want to, and Grandma won't let me say no. She says I have to try it for a week first."

"That actually sounds like a good idea," says Dad. "What do you say, Laurie?"

Mom looks at me, her eyes full of sympathy. I feel hopeful for a second, but then she turns back to the computer and says, "I do agree that Louie should at least give it a try before he decides not to do it."

Dad nods. "What do you say, Louie?"

My jaw drops. How could my dad agree with them? I thought Burger men always stuck together. I just need to speak to him alone. I know he'd change his mind if I could explain about the song.

"But, Dad," I say.

"I know I'd sure love to see you sing. Lots of comedians were great singers, too. Think about Groucho Marx."

That may be true, but I'm sure he never had to sing a song like this one.

"Okay, kids, I'm going to say good night to you now so I can talk to Mom alone for a little while."

"Good night, Daddy!" Ruby leans forward and kisses the computer, leaving a wet smudge on the screen. Gross.

" 'Night, Dad," Ari calls back over her shoulder. She's already walking out of the room and texting.

I straighten my back, still staring at the screen. It's not fair that Mom gets to talk to Dad alone and I don't. There are some things you can't say in front of moms.

"Did you want to tell Dad anything else?" Mom asks.

I stare into my dad's eyes on the computer, silently communicating that I really want to talk to him alone. If he were here, he'd understand. He's pretty good at reading my mind because of male bonding. I just hope the bond can stretch all the way through the computer.

"I'll be sitting in the front row, Louie. This really gives me something to look forward to when I get home! Love you, buddy."

My shoulders droop like someone rested a lead scarf across them. I guess our bond doesn't stretch that far. I wonder if I should demand to talk to

him alone, but then I decide it will be easier to send another e-mail.

"Bye," I say, turning and walking to my room to get ready for bed. I know everyone wants me to decide later, but the only thing I plan to decide is how to get out of singing.

To : dburger@email.com

I DON'T WANT TO SING

ATTACH **B** *I* U | Aa | ▣ | ✂ ✐ | ☰ ☰ | ☰ ☰ | ☺ | ∿ | 8:30pm

The song is about a boy who likes dolls. If I sing it everyone will think I like dolls. Also you said we would computer chat all the time, but I didn't even get to talk to you at all.

To : burgerboy@email.com

SORRY

ATTACH **B** *I* U | Aa | ▣ | ✂ ✐ | ☰ ☰ | ☰ ☰ | ☺ | ∿ | 10:30pm

No one will think you like dolls. It's just a song. Everyone will know that.

Let's try to chat again tomorrow.

INTERNATIONAL BOY DAY

On Thursday morning, I wake to the sound of Grandma singing again. *"R-E-S-P-E-C-T."* Her voice floats down the hall from the kitchen along with a sweet and sugary scent that makes me picture a bakery with platters of muffins and cakes and unlimited deliciousness. Uh-oh. I think she might be making her famous banana bread waffles. My mouth starts watering even though I already decided I'm not going to eat any of her food until she says I don't have to sing. My mouth is a traitor.

I stumble out of bed and into the bathroom, where I step on a unicorn that Ruby left right in the doorway.

"Ow!" I hop around on my left foot, rubbing the

sole of my right foot, trying to take away the pain. Sometimes I believe that unicorns are the most evil creatures on the planet. Right after sisters. If I had a little brother instead of a little sister, there would be no unicorns in my bathroom.

When my foot feels better, I use it to kick three unicorns across the bathroom floor. I send them skittering over the tiles to the corner behind the toilet, then I chuckle to myself. That seems like the perfect place for them.

I turn to the counter to brush my teeth, and it looks like a rainbow exploded. There are about thirty different kinds of makeup and things that look like paintbrushes and giant Q-tips everywhere. Everything is dusted with sparkly powder in different shades of blue, green, red, and purple. It's disgusting. I can barely see the countertop. And I can't find my toothbrush anywhere. Normally, I'd be happy to have an excuse not to have to brush my teeth, but today I am annoyed. Girls think they own the world.

"Ari," I shout. "I should throw all your makeup in the garbage. This isn't your own personal private bathroom, you know!"

I use my forearm to sweep the makeup to one side of the counter and find my toothbrush smashed beneath a container of Cheeky Cheeks blush. I squeeze on a dollop of toothpaste, and quickly brush my teeth. When I rinse my toothbrush afterward, I realize that the bristles are glittery pink. I rinse them again, but the pink hue doesn't get any lighter. The brush seems to be permanently dyed from the blush.

I check my smile in the mirror, and my heart skips a beat. My teeth are dyed pink, too.

I can't go to school with pink teeth.

I stagger backward away from the mirror, staring at my pink grimace. I know I've said it a million times, but sisters should be registered with the government as a form of torture. Nick and Henry never have to deal with this kind of stuff. I take another step backward, rubbing my teeth with my finger; maybe that will get the stain off. I take another step backward. From a distance my teeth don't look as pink as they used to. One more step back and— Whoa!

I trip over a unicorn that I missed before and fall into the shower curtain. I grab hold of it so I won't land in the bathtub, and slide twelve inches to the right as the curtain opens and a strange hat with earflaps falls on my head.

When the curtain has stopped sliding, I stand up and remove the hat. Then I look in the mirror and realize it wasn't a hat at all. I'm standing in the middle of a sparkle-explosion bathroom holding my grandma's jumbo old-lady brassiere. I fling it as far away as possible and run out of the bathroom. This is the most barfgusting thing that has ever happened to me. My skin crawls with girlzilla germs.

I know I'm not supposed to miss my father, but none of this would be happening if he was here. I don't know if I can take another week and a day without him. I finish getting dressed, then I march

into the kitchen and grab a Pop-Tart from the pantry.

"I made breakfast," my grandma says. "Put that back."

I bite off the corner and close my eyes to savor the sugar as I chew. "Dad lets me eat Pop-Tarts for breakfast."

Grandma makes her *tsk*ing noise again, then says, "Why do you want to eat that cardboard when there are fresh-baked strawberry heart-shaped pop-overs, scrambled eggs, and juicy orange slices?" She gestures at the table. Ari, who looks like she's wearing parrot-themed face paint, takes a bite of pop-over. "It's really delicious, Grandma."

Ruby smiles at me with an orange wedge stuck in her mouth. She says something, but it sounds all mumbly.

"I don't speak fruit," I tell her. "I'm going to eat outside while I wait for Nick. I want to walk to school today." I rush out the door before Grandma can stop me. While I'm waiting for Nick, I sit down on the front porch and write a new entry in my comedy journal. It's a video idea called *Boy vs. Brassiere*—based on a true story. I know I won't actually be able to make it, but at least I can imagine.

A little while later Grandma, Ari, and Ruby come outside and get into the pink Cadillac. Grandma looks at me carefully as she walks past me down the front steps. It's as if I'm some strange new creature she's never seen before and she's trying to decide if I bite. "Are you certain you don't want a ride?"

Princess wriggles out of Grandma's arms and scampers over to me. She drops her purple tiara chew toy next to my knee. I inch away from her doggy girlzilla germs.

"I prefer to walk."

When Nick and Henry finally come outside, I'm so excited to see them I practically tackle them.

"Hey," says Nick. "Are your teeth pink?"

I shake my head and pull my lips in tight. "Might be an optical illusion."

"Where's Ruby?" Henry asks as we start walking to school.

"She went in the girl-mobile," I tell him. "But that's okay because today is a new holiday. I just invented it. It's called International Boy Day. Here's how you celebrate: only talk to boys, do lots of boy things like spitting and telling jokes, and eat junk food."

Henry sticks out his tongue and blows a raspberry, then I show him how to really hock a loogie. I send a giant one right into a pile of leaves by the curb.

"Eww," he says. "Cool. I can't wait to tell Ruby about International Boy Day."

I shake my head. "You have to tell her tomorrow. No talking to girls today. Girls are barftrocious. Right, Nick?"

We turn the corner onto the last block before Barker Elementary.

"I guess," he says, raising one shoulder all the way up to his ear. "*Some* girls are barftrocious. Not all of them. I'm going to ask Ava to Go Out when we get to school."

I smack my palm against my forehead. "Weren't

you listening to anything I just said? Today is International Boy Day. You can't talk to her today."

"I have to. Thermos told Hannah to tell Ava that I am going to ask her before the bell rings." Nick pushes his glasses up the bridge of his nose. "International Boy Day isn't a real thing. You just made it up. But I won't talk to her after I ask her, okay?"

I shrug. If he asks her first it kind of defeats the whole purpose. I don't know why Nick doesn't get that. "Fine," I say.

"What about Thermos?" he asks as we hit the blacktop. We say goodbye to Henry and walk over to the fifth-grade area. "She's a girl. Are you going to ignore her all day? That's not very nice."

I shake my head. "We can talk to Thermos. She doesn't count. But she probably shouldn't talk to other girls."

I look over at Nick, ready for him to agree with me, but he's looking across the basketball court. "There's Ava," he says, pointing. He sets his backpack on the ground, wipes his palms on his jeans, then walks over to her without so much as a backward glance at me.

After a few seconds, I put my bag down and follow him to the basketball hoops. Ava and Hannah are watching Thermos and Jamal play H-O-R-S-E. Nick says something to Ava and she nods her head, then Nick starts playing H-O-R-S-E and Ava and Hannah start whispering.

I guess they are Going Out now. I don't see the big deal. It seems about the same as when they weren't Going Out.

"Hi, Louie," Jamal says when I get to the basketball court.

"Hey," I say.

"Hi," Thermos says, passing me the ball. "Your shot. Hopping. From the blue line."

"Okay," I say. I step up to the blue line, hop on one foot, and shoot the ball.

"Hi, Louie," Ava and Hannah call to me from the other side of the basketball court.

I pretend I don't hear them, catch my rebound, and announce, "Guess that's H."

"Hey, Louie," Hannah calls. "Tell Jamal I like his new jacket."

This is why the world needs International Boy Day. Why would Hannah tell me to tell Jamal that she likes his jacket when he's standing right next to me and heard her telling me to tell him and she could have easily told him herself? Girls make no sense! I stare off into the distance and pretend that all my attention is riveted by a cloud.

"Do you think it's going to rain?" I ask Jamal.

"It's going to be raining letters on your head when I beat you at H-O-R-S-E." Jamal is a master of trash talk. He shoots the ball from way beyond the three-point line. *Swish.* "That's what I'm talking about! Will you tell Hannah that that was a three-pointer? She wanted to know what a three-pointer was."

Not Jamal, too! This girl thing really *is* contagious.

I do not tell Hannah anything.

Thermos lines up and takes her shot. The ball hits the backboard, then sinks.

Nick catches the ball and lines up for his shot.

He shoots. The ball hits the front of the rim and bounces back to him. "That's H." He sighs.

"Good try!" Ava shouts from the bench next to the court.

"Thanks," Nick shouts back.

"Ni-ick," I say through clenched teeth. Has he already forgotten about International Boy Day?

Nick looks at me, shrugs, and passes the ball.

I take my shot and miss. Total air ball. H-O.

"Good try, Louie!" Hannah shouts. "Tell Jamal good luck on his next shot."

I pass Jamal the ball, but don't tell him anything. Then I bend down and retie my shoes. When I stand back up, Thermos is right next to me, holding the basketball.

"What's up?" she asks.

I point. "The sky."

"Ha-ha." She folds her arms across her chest and raises an eyebrow. "Seriously. You are acting weird today. You are barely talking to anyone."

"They don't need me to tell everyone everything. They can all hear each other just fine."

Thermos shrugs, tucks the basketball against her hip, and scuffs her shoe on the court. "Sometimes it's hard to talk to someone you like."

"Why does everyone have to like someone?" Her words make my back itch. I squirm around, trying to get the funny feeling off my shoulder blades. "Besides, I'm not talking to girls today. It's International Boy Day."

Thermos wrinkles her forehead and stares hard at me with one eye. "International *Boy* Day?"

"I invented it. Because of the girlzilla infestation at my house. It's a day for boys to be free from girls. They don't have to talk to girls all day long and they do boy stuff like spitting and eating junk food."

Thermos barks out a laugh. "Good one."

"It's not a joke," I tell her.

"Then that is the dumbest thing I have ever heard in the whole history of dumb things. First of all, spitting and junk food are not boy things. They are people things. My favorite food after soup is Ho Hos." Then she wiggles her jaw for a few seconds, sucks in her cheeks, and lets a huge gobber of saliva fly across the blacktop. "Second of all, I spit better than anyone in our whole grade. And third of all, you're talking to me, so how could it really be International Boy Day?"

Thermos juts her chin out at me after she finishes talking as if she really proved her point.

I smile. It's simple. "It *is* International Boy Day," I tell her. "The reason you like Ho Hos and can spit so far is the same reason I can talk to you. You aren't really a girl. You're an honorary boy. You should stop talking to girls today, too."

Thermos presses her lips together and stares at me coldly for a minute. I feel my smile waver. I don't know what she's getting worked up about. "That was a compliment," I explain.

Thermos narrows her eyes. "I was wrong. You aren't becoming like Ryan Rakefield. You are becoming worse. And you have pink teeth!" My hands fly up to my mouth as Thermos passes the ball to me, hard. It knocks me backward. "I don't feel like playing anymore," she tells Nick and Jamal. "I'll catch you later."

I watch Thermos stomp over to the swings, where she sits down and gives me the evil eye, even though all I did was try to say something nice. Ava and Hannah both give me girlzilla glares and storm off to sit next to Thermos.

I wonder if I was wrong about her. Maybe she really is a girl. Gross.

ALMOST INTERNATIONAL BOYS ARE STUPID DAY

Thermos doesn't sit with me, Nick, and Jamal at lunch. She sits near Ava, Hannah, Violet, and a bunch of other girls. But I don't look at them. I added another rule to International Boy Day. No looking at girls. Not even a glance or a peek. Nick keeps breaking it.

"Sometimes you're pretty dumb." He takes a bite of his baloney sandwich.

"It was a compliment. She should feel flattered, not angry," I tell him. I open my lunch box, fish out the turkey sandwich my grandmother made, and hold it up to Nick. She cut it in the shape of a heart. Barf. "What will you give me for this?"

Nick rolls his apple across the table. A sandwich

for an apple is not the best trade I've ever made, but I am not going to eat anything girly. I hand him the Baggie and crunch into the apple.

"Hey, Nick," Jamal says. "Will you ask Ava to ask Hannah what she would say if someone asked her who she likes?"

Nick holds my turkey sandwich in one hand and his baloney sandwich in the other. He takes a bite of each, then says, "Sure," with his mouth full.

I'm surrounded by traitors.

"The whole reason we hang out with Thermos is because she's not like a girl. It's the whole reason she hangs out with us, too. Otherwise she'd be sitting over there every day." I nod back toward where the girls are sitting. "I don't see why she's so mad."

Nick looks up like he's about to answer, then his eyes widen. He stares at something just past my shoulder.

"Uh-oh." Jamal squinches up his eyes and shakes his head.

I turn around and see Thermos and all the girls

from her new table marching toward us. Thermos doesn't look happy.

"We would like you to know," she says, "that today might be International Boy Day, but tomorrow is International Boys Are Stupid Day. Happy Almost International Boys Are Stupid Day."

Thermos gives me a dirty look, then walks past me to throw away her trash. One by one all the girls file past, saying, "Happy Almost International Boys Are Stupid Day." Except Ava, who says, "Happy Almost International Boys Are Stupid Day. Hi, Nick." And Hannah, who says, "Happy Almost International Boys Are Stupid Day. Louie, would you please tell Jamal I am not going to say hi to him tomorrow."

I open my mouth to remind her that she technically didn't even say hi to him today, but then I remember my rules and shut it fast before I accidentally break them.

Nick gives Ava a half smile and calls out after her, "Hi."

I kick him under the table.

"What?" Nick shrugs and looks sheepish. "I have to say hi to her. We're Going Out."

"But you are a boy," I remind him. "And she's celebrating International Boys Are Stupid Day."

"Only because you started it with International

Boy Day. I don't want to spend a whole day not talking to girls. I don't think girls are that bad."

I finish my apple, then pull one of Grandma's homemade chocolate chip cookies out of my lunch box. It smells really chocolaty, and I can tell from the way it squishes between my fingers that it will be chewy, not crunchy, which is just the way I like it. But I won't eat it. It's covered with red and purple sprinkles. I pass it to Jamal, who grabs it and gives me his Baggie of carrot sticks.

Carrot sticks.

I pull one out and take a bite. "You guys only think girls aren't bad because you don't have to live with five of them."

"Don't you mean four?" Jamal asks.

I shake my head. "Don't forget Princess."

Nick sighs. "Girls are 50 percent of the world, and I like eating lunch with Thermos. Can't you tell her you're sorry so we can go back to normal?"

I crunch another carrot stick and watch Jamal take a chewy gooey bite of chocolate chip cookie. A little trail of melted chocolate hangs on his bottom lip and he licks it up. Grandma makes the world's best chocolate chip cookies. "Maybe," I tell him. "I'll think about it."

That afternoon, just before we go to our lockers to pack up, Mrs. Adler stops in the doorway. "Don't forget, everyone, tonight is Growing Up Night. I look forward to seeing you and all of your special adult guests this evening."

I forgot about Growing Up Night! As my class walks into the hallway, I realize there is finally one good thing about my dad being out of town. We never did come up with a plan, so I won't have to go!

At my locker, I silently pack up my bag next to Thermos as she silently packs up hers. I miss the way we usually joke around at the end of the day. I zip my backpack, close my locker, and stand there, trying to think of how to apologize.

When Thermos finishes packing her bag she turns around and notices me standing behind her, waiting.

"What?" she says, putting her hands on her hips.

I open my mouth to say something, but I still haven't thought of an apology. Thermos can be kind of scary when she's mad at you.

"Aren't you going to say anything?" She taps her foot a couple times.

My brain flashes all my options: *You* are *a girl, just not the bad kind. I'm sorry you are a girl. I still want to be friends even though you are a girl.* They all sound okay to me, but I'm worried they will make Thermos even madder. So I stand there with my mouth hanging open. All that comes out is a small squeak.

Thermos snorts. "Oh, I get it. Now you're not talking to me either? Well, guess what, I have news for you. If you think I'm not a real girl just because I won't wear hair bows and I like to play sports, then you must not be a real boy because you don't like sports at all and you keep your room really, really neat."

Thermos's words hit me in the face like a banana cream pie. I don't keep my room really, *really* neat. I just like my comedy stuff to be organized, that's all, so I can find my rubber chickens and whoopee cushions when I need them. And sports are boring and dangerous. Only crazy people like sports. Those things don't mean I'm not a boy.

"Happy Almost International Boys Are Stupid Day," Thermos says as she turns and leaves me in the hallway.

Only when she's gone do I realize that she shouldn't wish me Happy International Boys Are Stupid Day if she thinks I'm not a real boy. Somehow though, the thought doesn't make me feel better. I start walking the other way down the hallway to meet Nick when I'm stopped by Ryan Rakefield. I sigh. I'm not in the mood to ignore his teasing, but I pick an answer anyway. Whatever he says, I'm going to moo.

"Hey, Louie," he says. "What's International Boy Day?"

That's strange. Ryan used my actual name. Not a weird insult nickname.

"Moo," I answer.

"No, seriously. I want to know what it is."

I shrug. This has to be a joke. But none of Ryan's cronies are here to watch. He usually prefers to tease with an audience. I don't even know how Ryan heard of International Boy Day. He's probably going to tell me how dumb it is, so it would be totally stupid to answer him, but I do anyway. "It's a holiday I invented. No talking to girls. Lots of spitting, telling jokes, and eating junk food."

Ryan nods. "Good idea," he says, then he walks away.

Now I'm really confused. The evidence doesn't add up.

Girlzillas are driving me crazy, therefore International Boy Day is good.

It makes Thermos mad. Therefore International Boy Day is bad.

Ryan says International Boy Day is good. But Ryan is a jerk face.

I don't know what to think. Then an awful thought pops into my head again. If I were a girl, I wouldn't have to deal with any of this mess. I could eat heart sandwiches and pink cookies and be friends with Thermos and never play sports and keep my room as neat as I like. Everything would be easier and less confusing.

It's not fair. Girls have it made.

GROWING, GROWING, GROAN

After dinner, Mom asks me to help her clear the dishes.

"But it's not my turn," I remind her. "It's not your turn either. Why isn't Ari doing her job?" I give Ari a dirty look, and she gives me her trademark snotty smile.

"Come on, Ruby," Ari says. "Let's go play unicorns."

Ari gives me a little wave as she and Ruby walk out of the kitchen, and Mom hands me two glasses to take to the sink.

"I'm going to freshen up." Grandma takes her own dishes to the sink, then hums quietly to herself as she dances out the doorway.

"I know it's supposed to be Ari's turn," Mom says, "but I'm taking over as a favor. Ari is babysitting Ruby tonight since I have to run the informational meeting for freshman volleyball and you have Growing Up Night."

Mom stacks the rest of the plates in a pile and carries them over to the counter. I put the glasses next to the sink and slowly turn around.

"But Dad is out of town," I tell her. "We never came up with a backup plan. I can't go to Growing Up Night alone. And why can't Grandma babysit—"

I stop. Mom looks at me guiltily from across the table where she has stacked the green bean bowl on top of the salad bowl. "No way." I shake my head. "No way."

Mom puts the two bowls back down on the table. "Grandma is not going to take you for the whole thing. She is just going to drive you and Nick, and then Mr. Yamashita will meet you there. He said he'd be happy to be your dad for the night."

"Growing Up Night is not that big a deal," I tell her. "I can miss it."

"Growing Up Night is a very big deal," she tells me. "How would it look to the other teachers in the district if I let my kid miss important activities? You are going to learn a lot, and then you and your father can have an extra-special bonding time when he gets home."

I keep shaking my head. Maybe this is a nightmare. I shout the words *wake up* inside my head, but nothing changes. I'm *still* standing in the kitchen. And I still have to go to Growing Up Night.

Mom passes me two more glasses for the sink. I hear Grandma humming from the bathroom down the hall. Growing Up Night all by itself is horrible. But driving to Growing Up Night with your grandma? Barfmiliating.

o o o

When Grandma, Nick, and I arrive at school, Mrs. Adler and Principal Newton greet us in the lobby.

"Mr. Burger! Mr. Yamashita!" Principal Newton steps up to us and clasps his hands behind his back. He's always keeping his hands behind his back.

Sometimes I wonder if maybe he's hiding something. "Please introduce us to your special guest."

"Yes." Mrs. Adler puts her hand on my arm and smiles at me. "Hello, Louie. Hello, Nick. I'd love to know who you've brought tonight."

I sigh. "This is my grandma. She's not staying."

"She's waiting with us until my dad gets here," Nick explains.

Grandma shakes hands with Mrs. Adler and Principal Newton. "Josephine Gorden," she says. "Nice to meet you."

"Where's your grandpa?" a loud voice barks behind me. I freeze. He wouldn't make fun of me for bringing my grandmother in front of grownups, would he?

I turn to look and see Ryan Rakefield standing next to a giant. Maybe not really a giant, but seriously, the guy is about a mile tall and shaped like a tree trunk. The man clamps a huge, Frankenstein-sized hand on Ryan's shoulder and squeezes. "Don't interrupt," the giant orders out of the side of his mouth.

Ryan scowls and stares at the carpet. I close
my eyes and wish I could sink through the floor.

"Ron Rakefield," the giant says. He shakes hands with everyone.

"Ryan," Mrs. Adler says, "why don't you show your dad to the gym?"

They walk down the hall to the right, and Nick stands by the door to look for his dad.

I hear a faint buzzing noise. "Excuse me," says my grandmother, holding up her phone. "I need to take this."

Great. Just what we need. Makeup talk. She should head over to the girls' room.

"Theodora!" Mrs. Adler says, looking over my shoulder. My heartbeat speeds up at the sound of Thermos's name. I want to say hi, or do *something* that will end our fight. "Who did you bring tonight?"

I turn around, and then I freeze.

"This is my aunt Lisa," Thermos says. Aunt Lisa still looks kind of like an uncle. She is wearing torn blue jeans and purple sneakers and a green T-shirt that says: *Everything Is Easier Said Than Done. Except for Talking. That's About the Same.* She looks at me and gives me a funny smile. I wonder if she told Thermos about the football game. About Joe thinking I was a girl. Is that why Thermos told me I wasn't really a boy?

I look over at Thermos. She's frowning at me. I open my mouth to speak, but I still can't think of anything to say and Aunt Lisa is watching me very carefully.

Grandma steps back over next to me and says, "No. Of course. I understand," into the phone. Then she says, "I will let them know. Goodbye."

Nick is still looking at the parking lot when Grandma calls him over. My dinner starts to churn in my stomach.

"Nick, your father is stuck in traffic. He's not going to be here for a while."

Nick's face falls, and he looks at me like he wants me to do something, but what can I do?

"I guess we'll have to miss it?" I suggest.

"Nonsense," says Principal Newton. "Your grand-mother can take you boys in until Mr. Yamashita arrives. We've had mothers attend in the past."

There is a big difference between mothers and

grandmothers. Thermos gives me a look of horror, and for one second I think maybe she's not mad at me. But then her face goes blank and she looks away.

"Theodora, why don't you show Aunt Lisa to the cafeteria?" Mrs. Adler gestures the other way down the hallway. Thermos walks away with her aunt.

"Louie, Nick, I'll make sure Mr. Yamashita finds you right away as soon as he arrives. I'm sure it won't be too long."

Nick nods, but I'll bet he's thinking what I'm thinking. One second of Growing Up Night with my grandma is one second too long.

We walk to the gym, and I try to stay ahead with Nick so no one will know we are with my grandma. When we get to the gym, there is a microphone and a big white screen set up under the scoreboard and rows and rows of chairs. Most of them are already filled, so Grandma suggests we split up to see if we can find seats. She heads up the center aisle straight for the front row. As my grandma walks to the front of the gym, every single set of eyeballs turns to look.

They scan the room, trying to figure out who's the kid who brought a *grandma*.

Jamal and his dad are sitting in the middle of the gym. He waves to Nick and me, so we go say hi.

"Where are your dads?"

"Mine's stuck in traffic," Nick says.

"Out of town," I say. I don't say anything about my grandma.

Then Jamal's dad says, "We've got an extra seat here if one of you wants it."

"Do you?" Nick asks.

"You can take it." I feel like I owe him one. I slink over to a corner seat near the back row, and scrunch myself way down small. Maybe no one will notice me, and Grandma will find a seat on the opposite side of the gym.

"Louuu-ie!" I scrunch down lower, but let my eyes look up. Grandma is standing at the front of the room, practically next to the microphone, shouting for me. "Louuu-ie! I found seats!"

Other people start to look around for me, too. I'm obviously not going to be able to hide here forever, so I stand up and wave until my grandmother sees me, then I sit back down.

Grandma winds her way over to me. "Where's Nick? Why are you sitting all the way back here? If you scoot any farther backward, you'll be in the hallway."

"Sounds good to me," I say under my breath. Then louder, "Nick's sitting with Jamal."

"Gentlemen, please have a seat. We are going to get started." A man in blue hospital scrubs stands at the mike. "Oh, excuse me," he says, looking over at my corner of the room. "Gentlemen and lady. I'm glad we have at least one woman brave enough to join us tonight."

Grandma bustles past me and asks the people next to us if they will shift over one seat so she can sit in the seat next to mine.

"Hi, everyone," says the man at the mike. "I'm Hector, and I'm looking forward to talking to you tonight. We're going to start off with a fun and informative video, then I will talk for a little bit, then I will answer your questions." Hector points to the back of the room. I turn around and see Principal Newton and Mr. Lamb, our gym teacher, standing on either side of a small table. "Some of your teachers are standing by the question box. Any time you have a question tonight write it down and slip it in the box. There are pencils and paper under your chairs. No one has to be embarrassed, and no one has to know who asked what."

Hector steps away from the mike and hits the lights. A cartoon movie appears on the screen and the characters tell us that we are all going to get pimples and have funny-sounding voices. Some of us will get really tall, but some of us might stay shrimps practically forever. Oh, and for the next few years we will need lots of sleep and we will be in a bad mood most of the time.

The lights come back on and Hector says, "How many of you want to go to Neverland so you won't grow up?"

A couple of dads raise their hands and laugh. Most of the boys shift in their seats. I try to tap my toes on the floor and realize that my feet don't reach all the way if I'm sitting back in my chair. I wonder if that means I'm going to be one of those boys who stays short forever. Maybe *that's* why Mrs. Lineball wanted me to sing about a little boy who likes dolls.

"That movie makes it sound pretty bad, but there's also a lot of cool stuff about growing up." Hector tells us about getting strong muscles and getting smarter, and then he says it's time for questions. A bunch of people reach down under their chairs and start writing, so I do, too.

I pull the paper out and wonder which of the five hundred questions I should ask. *Is it dangerous for a boy to live in a house with only girls? What does it mean if a teacher wants you to sing a song about dolls? Why is being a girl so much easier than being a boy?*

Finally I think of a really good one, and I write it down. *Why do girls get mad at you when you didn't even do anything wrong?*

"What's your question?" Grandma asks, leaning over and trying to get a peek at my paper. I fold it up quickly. She hands me her slip of paper. "Take mine to the box, too."

Her paper isn't folded, so I read her question. *Is it important for boys to have a relationship with their grandmothers?*

I groan. Everyone is going to know that question is about us. I tuck Grandma's question in my back pocket and put my own in the box. Then I grab some boring sugar cookies from the refreshment table (they are the only flavor the PTA ever serves) and go back to my seat.

Grandma holds out her hand for a cookie, and I pass her one. She takes a bite and makes a face. "Store bought."

I take a bite, too. The cookies don't really taste so great, but I don't know how Grandma can tell they are store bought. Maybe they just taste bad because they are sugar cookies.

Principal Newton carries the box of questions to Hector, who steps back to the mike. "Okay, everyone, please take your seats again, and feel free to grab a few more cookies."

He sets the box on a little table, removes the lid, then swishes his hand around inside before pulling out the first question. He unfolds the paper slowly.

"Good first question. *How do you pop a zit?*"

A bunch of boys laugh. I start to chuckle, but then I look up at Grandma. She's pressing her lips tightly together. She turns her head toward me, so I quickly look back at Hector.

"When you get a pimple, it's really tempting to pop it or squeeze it till some gunk comes out. I know, I know. It sounds like a monster movie. Here's what I have to say: *Don't do it!* When you squeeze a pimple, some stuff comes out, but more stuff goes deeper into your skin. It could get infected and even leave a scar. So keep your face clean and keep your hands at your sides. Although you might stop at the drugstore for some cover-up. Yes, boys can wear cover-up."

Grandma leans over to me. "I can get you some great Flashy Face cover-up if you want."

"No!" I whisper-shout, and the dad in front of me turns around to look. I lower my voice. "No makeup!"

I check the clock above Hector's head. There are still fifteen minutes to go. I don't know why we can't leave right now. Ari is the only one in my family who gets pimples.

"Next question. *Why do girls get mad at you when you didn't even do anything wrong?*"

A bunch of dads crack up when Hector reads my question, which makes no sense because it isn't a joke. I feel my cheeks burst into flame. I'm sure everyone in the room knows that I wrote it. I hold myself perfectly still. Did Grandma just look at me?

"This question's a doozy." Hector smiles. "Sometimes girls can be pretty hard to understand. That's why they are all in the room down the hall."

More people laugh, and not just the dads, but I don't. I feel like the screen next to Hector has a big sign on it that says: *Louie's Question!*

"Sometimes in fifth grade, boys' and girls' friendships start changing. It can get pretty confusing to know how to act around each other. But it's completely normal to have a crush on a girl," Hector says.

Wait. *What?*

Why would he be saying that? My heartbeat starts to pick up speed. I didn't ask anything about crushes.

"Sometimes when a girl gets mad, it might mean she has a crush on you, too. But sometimes it just means you did something dumb."

What is he talking about? I don't have a crush on Thermos. She's my best friend. Did he just say Thermos has a crush on me?

"Even though you might like someone in fifth grade, and she might like you back, it's smart to wait until you are in high school to start dating. Dating takes a lot of emotional maturity and growing up before you are ready to do it. So for now, if you like somebody, try to become *friends*. That's the most important part of dating anyway."

Hector reaches into the box for the next question, but I don't pay any attention when he reads it. My ears are filled with the rush of my pulse and my brain is filled with the rush of my thoughts, circling around and around, even when Hector finishes talking and we stand up to go home.

My question didn't say anything about dating.

Thermos thinks dating is gross.

I think dating is gross.

I just wanted to know why Thermos got angry, because I can't see any reason. But if there is no reason, then maybe Hector is right. Maybe Thermos—

Oh no.

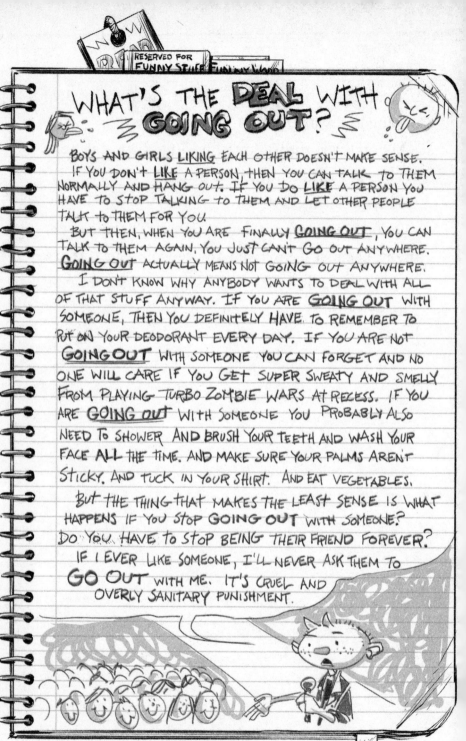

WHAT'S THE DEAL WITH GOING OUT?

BOYS AND GIRLS LIKING EACH OTHER DOESN'T MAKE SENSE. IF YOU DON'T LIKE A PERSON, THEN YOU CAN TALK TO THEM NORMALLY AND HANG OUT. IF YOU DO LIKE A PERSON YOU HAVE TO STOP TALKING TO THEM AND LET OTHER PEOPLE TALK TO THEM FOR YOU.

BUT THEN, WHEN YOU ARE FINALLY GOING OUT, YOU CAN TALK TO THEM AGAIN. YOU JUST CAN'T GO OUT ANYWHERE. GOING OUT ACTUALLY MEANS NOT GOING OUT ANYWHERE.

I DON'T KNOW WHY ANYBODY WANTS TO DEAL WITH ALL OF THAT STUFF ANYWAY. IF YOU ARE GOING OUT WITH SOMEONE, THEN YOU DEFINITELY HAVE TO REMEMBER TO PUT ON YOUR DEODORANT EVERY DAY. IF YOU ARE NOT GOING OUT WITH SOMEONE YOU CAN FORGET AND NO ONE WILL CARE IF YOU GET SUPER SWEATY AND SMELLY FROM PLAYING TURBO ZOMBIE WARS AT RECESS. IF YOU ARE GOING OUT WITH SOMEONE YOU PROBABLY ALSO NEED TO SHOWER AND BRUSH YOUR TEETH AND WASH YOUR FACE ALL THE TIME. AND MAKE SURE YOUR PALMS AREN'T STICKY. AND TUCK IN YOUR SHIRT. AND EAT VEGETABLES.

BUT THE THING THAT MAKES THE LEAST SENSE IS WHAT HAPPENS IF YOU STOP GOING OUT WITH SOMEONE? DO YOU HAVE TO STOP BEING THEIR FRIEND FOREVER?

IF I EVER LIKE SOMEONE, I'LL NEVER ASK THEM TO GO OUT WITH ME. IT'S CRUEL AND OVERLY SANITARY PUNISHMENT.

MAJOR. BRAIN. FREEZE.

"I could use an ice cream sundae," Grandma says when we get into her car after Growing Up Night. Nick's dad showed up right at the end, so he took Nick home himself. "How about we go to Frosty House, just the two of us?"

I buckle my seat belt and think about it. On the one hand, I don't want even more people to see me with my grandma on Growing Up Night, but on the other hand Frosty House does smush-ins with Marshmallow Fluff and gummy bears.

"Okay," I say. "I guess."

When we get to Frosty House, Grant, Owen, Hannah, and a bunch of kids from the other fifth-grade classes are already sitting at tables. Grandma and I stand in line to place our order, and after we get our plastic number card, we find a table in the corner and sit down.

"What did you think?" Grandma asks.

I shrug. "It was pretty weird."

Grandma nods. "Yep."

"I already own deodorant, anyway."

Grandma nods and pushes out her lips like she's impressed. "What about girls?" she asks.

"They're stupid," I tell her. "Except . . ." I almost say Thermos, but then I'll have to explain what happened between us. And right now, I'm a little confused about that.

Grandma laughs. "I'm a girl and I'm not stupid. What about your mom and your sisters? They aren't stupid."

I tilt my head and think about it for a while. "I guess my *mom* isn't stupid," I finally say.

A Frosty House server steps up to our table. "Who had the hot fudge?"

Grandma raises her hand, and the server sets

the sundae in front of her and my smush-in in front of me.

When Grandma eats a big gooey spoonful of ice cream, she closes her eyes and says, "Mmmm."

A bell jingles over the doorway. I look up and see Thermos walk in with her aunt. Instantly my cheeks feel radioactive. They could probably melt my ice cream. I hope Hector wasn't right. What if Thermos asked a question about me and *her* nurse told Thermos I like her? This is too weird. I just want to make up and be friends again, but how can I talk to her if I don't know what she's thinking?

I stare into my dish and count the gummy bears. I'm up to seven before I let myself take another peek at Thermos. When I look up, she's looking at me, so I quickly look down again.

"Somehow I feel we've gotten off on the wrong foot," Grandma says. "Did I do something to upset you?"

"Huh?" I look at my grandmother, but I have a hard time focusing on her words. I can hear Thermos placing her order at the counter, but I don't even need to hear her to know that she's getting a root beer float. She always gets a root beer float when she goes out for ice cream.

"I thought of something we could do together that I think you would call really barfterastic. Is that the word? Anyway, I bought some DVDs I think you will like. Maybe we can watch them together."

"Mmmhmm," I say absentmindedly. Thermos's aunt starts walking toward the table next to ours, but Thermos tugs her sleeve and leads her to a table on the opposite side of the ice cream parlor.

"And I'm going to check out the video of *Free to*

Be . . . You and Me from the library. I think that will be fun for your sisters, too."

"Muh-huh," I say, hoping my mumbles will convince Grandma I'm actually listening to what she says. Thermos sits down at her table and looks over at me. I quickly look away and take a huge bite of ice cream. Then I get a brain freeze and look back at Thermos. As soon as she sees me looking, she looks away and laughs at something her aunt Lisa says.

I hope Aunt Lisa wasn't talking about me.

"That hit the spot." Grandma pushes the rest of her ice cream to the center of the table and rubs her stomach. "Now what's so interesting on the other side of the room that you keep staring at?"

I follow her eyes as they scan the other side of the room. Will she remember Thermos and Aunt Lisa from the school lobby? I can't risk it. I spoon what's left of my ice cream into my mouth all at once. I have to stretch my jaw as far as it will go. The frozen gummy bears stick to my teeth as the ice cream melts and slides down my throat.

Major. Brain. Freeze.

I put my hand on my forehead. Ow. "I'm done. We can go home now."

Grandma *tsk*s at me. "There was no hurry. I would have waited for you to finish."

We stand, Grandma hooks her purse over her arm, and I watch Thermos out of the corner of my eye as I step up to the door of Frosty House. Thermos leans forward, cups her hand around the side of her mouth, and says something to her aunt, who turns and watches me as I go.

I casually pull on the door handle like I can't tell I'm being watched, but it's stuck. I pull again, harder, but it still won't budge. I try two hands, and feel the back of my neck and ears tingle because I know Thermos and her aunt must think I'm a weakling. Thermos could probably open the door with her pinkie.

"It says 'push,'" Grandma whispers in my ear.

I look at the door and notice the little black-and-gold sign above the handle. I give the door a push and it swings easily. Grandma and I walk outside, and the cold air soothes my embarrassment.

When we get home, I ask Grandma if I can computer chat with my dad. She looks at her watch. "It's an hour later over there. I don't know if he'll still be up, but you can try. Don't talk too long, though, it's nearly ten. You've got to get to bed."

She leaves me alone in the family room and goes to check on my sisters. I open up the computer-chat program and type in Dad's user name. Then I wait. The computer makes a *ping . . . ping . . . ping . . .* sound. I know that's the sound Dad's computer is making, too, and it feels nice to know we're already connected, even if it's only in a tiny way. Then I remember that his computer might be turned off.

The pings go on and on, and I guess I have to accept that my dad's not going to answer. I'm about to hit the disconnect button when the pings stop, and Dad's scruffy face appears in a little box in the top left corner of the screen. He has bedhead.

"Hey, Louie? Is that you?" His voice sounds scratchy and sleepy. "Is everything okay?"

No. Everything is not okay. I haven't figured out a way to get out of the Fifth-Grade Sing. My house is full of girlzillas, and I'm in a fight with Thermos. My dad wants me to be the man of the house, but I'm not even sure I know how to be a fifth-grade boy.

"Tonight was Growing Up Night," I remind him.

"Right." He rubs one eye with the palm of his hand. "How'd it go?"

"Barfominable." I rest my chin on my knuckles.

Dad puts his elbow on his desk and leans his cheek against his palm. "What made it so bad?"

"For one thing I had to go with"—I look over my shoulder to make sure no one is in the room with me, then I turn back to my dad and whisper—"with Grandma."

Dad smiles and lets his eyes close for a moment. Then he looks at me again. "Okay, that's not so great. What else?"

"It was just stupid. The guy told us stuff no one

even cares about, like popping pimples and liking girls."

"Well, you might not care about it now, but I can guarantee—" All of a sudden Dad stops talking and lets out a huge yawn. Then I yawn, too, because I guess yawns are contagious even through computer screens. "Sorry, Louie, I had a really long day. I know Growing Up Night was probably uncomfortable and yucky, and I wish I could have gone with you. We'll have a long talk about it when I get home, okay?"

I nod and shrug at the same time.

"I'm sorry, buddy, but I've got to go back to sleep. I have a really early morning tomorrow. You should get some sleep, too."

I hear Mom's car in the driveway. The engine turns off and the car door opens and shuts.

"Mom just got home," I tell him. "Do you want to wait and say hi to her?"

He yawns again. "I talked to her earlier. You tell her I said good night, okay? Bye."

I watch Dad push a button, then his face

disappears and my computer makes a *woop* sound. Behind me, I hear the side door of our house open.

"Louie!" My mother drops her purse on the little table next to the door and hangs her coat on the hook on the wall. "What are you still doing up?"

"I was talking with Dad." I power off the computer and slide back my chair. "He told me to tell you good night."

My mother and I walk out of the family room together and down the hall toward our bedrooms. "That was a great idea to call him. I bet it was almost like he was at Growing Up Night with you."

I look up at my mom. She has puffy circles under her eyes, and her eyelids are droopy. She yawns and rubs the side of her head just like my dad. "Yeah, almost," I say, even though it was nothing like he was there. "Good night."

I head into my bedroom and shut the door behind me.

I take off my shoe and hold it up like it's a microphone. Then I stand on top of my bed.

"What's the deal with growing up? Why is up the only direction? What if I wanted to grow down or grow out or grow around or grow under? I think it should be my own choice, you know?

"And why does it have to be so disgusting? Maybe it's to balance out all the cool things you get to do. Like, when you're a grownup you can eat Marshmallow Fluff for breakfast every day. That's cool.

But your armpits and nostrils grow hair. That's disgusting. When you are grown up, you don't have to ask permission to watch TV. That's cool. But the hair on your head falls out and your stomach pooches like a balloon. That's disgusting.

"If you ask me, grownups make too big a deal about growing up. Everything on the whole earth grows, and humans are the only species that thinks we need to watch a cartoon to do it right, like if I missed the movie maybe my mustache would grow on my ear instead of my upper lip."

I flop back down on my bed and let my shoecrophone drop to the floor. Then I drag myself to the Girlzilla Bathroom of Doom and get ready for bed.

INTERNATIONAL BOYS ARE STUPID DAY

I almost forgot that it was International Boys Are Stupid Day. (Which is *really* not a real holiday, by the way.) When I woke up this morning, I'd practically even forgotten that yesterday was International Boy Day. Nick and I didn't talk about it on the way to school. We talked about ideas for my next viral video. I was thinking I might do a remake. For example, I could do a remake of *Godzilla*, but call it *Girlzilla*. I could do a remake of *Toy Story* and call it *Boy Story*. Or I could do a remake of *Sleeping Beauty* called *Sleeping Doody*.

We had tons of good ideas, but they slide right out of my brain when I get to the blacktop before school and see Thermos playing four square with a group of girls. They are all wearing red circle-shaped stickers that say *Girls Rule!*

Nick looks at me and shakes his head.

"What?" I shrug my shoulders with my hands out in the air. "This isn't my fault."

Nick looks at me doubtfully. "It sort of is."

I sigh. Okay, fine, International Boy Day was my idea, but I only got the idea because of the girlzilla invasion at my house. How is *that* my fault? "What do you want me to do?"

"You could say you're sorry to Thermos." Nick puts his bag down and waves to Ava. She looks around to make sure none of the other girls are looking, then she gives Nick a little finger wiggle without raising her hand.

I put my backpack next to Nick's and we head over to the four-square court. "Thermos!" I call out when we get close. "Can I talk to you for a second?"

Thermos waits until the ball bounces out of bounds, then she stops the game and turns to me, one hand on her hip. The other girls on the court put their hands on their hips, too. "Sure. Just as soon as you say that there is nothing wrong with being a girl."

I swallow. All the girls are staring at me. "Um." My voice squeaks, and I clear my throat. "There is nothing wrong with being a girl?"

Thermos folds her arms across her chest and shakes her head at me. "You have to say it like you believe it."

Okay. I look around at the faces of the girls staring at me with their arms folded across their chests just below their red *Girls Rule!* circles. Waiting.

I take a deep breath. "There's nothing *wrong* with being a girl. I mean, I don't understand makeup or princess movies or giggling when nothing is funny. But you guys probably don't understand bobbleheads or Lou Lafferman or stand-up comedy or—*ow!*"

I turn to Nick, who has just elbowed me in the ribs. "What was that for?" I ask in a hushed voice.

"You need to stop talking," he tells me. "You're not making it better."

I look back at the girls and see squinty eyes, jutted jaws, and a lot of angry faces.

"But they don't watch Lou Lafferman," I remind him. "Why would they be mad at me for saying so?"

"Louie thinks girls don't know how to be funny." Thermos bounces the kick ball twice, then catches it. She looks around at all the girls playing four square, and they mumble sounds of annoyance.

Nick prods my back. "Just say you're sorry."

"Sorry?" I say.

Thermos stares at me. "Girls can be just as funny as boys."

I don't know about funny, but they can be plenty scary.

"You think *you* could be funnier than *Louie*?" a voice from behind me calls out.

My heart stops. I know that voice, but it couldn't be. I slowly turn to look, and sure enough, there is Ryan Rakefield.

"No way," Ryan says. "There's no way a *girl* could be funnier than Louie."

I feel like my brain is splitting in half. Ryan Rakefield is sticking up for me. Against Thermos. I don't know if I should feel good or bad.

Since when does Ryan Rakefield think I am

funny? And how did this situation get so messed up that Ryan and I are on one side and Thermos is on the other?

"I can so," says Thermos. "I can be way funnier."

"Prove it," Ryan says. "You and Louie will tell your best jokes after school and we'll see who's funnier."

Thermos blinks slowly, but other than that, she doesn't react. "Fine."

"Wait a minute!" I turn and face Ryan. I don't want a comedy war with Thermos. I wanted to make up. "I can't perform this afternoon."

"Okay, fine," Ryan says. "When do you want to do it? Monday? Tuesday? Wednesday?"

I turn pleading eyes to Thermos. I doubt she wants to do this any more than I do.

She swallows and looks at Ryan. "How about Thursday?"

Thermos walks over to the swings, and the girls follow. They huddle around her.

I look at Ryan. He smiles at me, but my stomach

lurches like he socked me in the gut. "How about February 31st? I don't want to have a comedy show-down," I tell him.

"You've got to," he says. "We can't let the girls win. Did you know they are pretending today is some kind of holiday about how girls are better than boys? I'm going to tell the guys. We'll be rooting for you. Hey, Owen!" Ryan heads over to Owen, and I turn to Nick.

"What should I do?"

Nick blinks at me a couple of times. "Move to Kalamazoo?"

The bell rings and the girls make sure they are in the front half of the line. Ava is the very last girl, and Nick gets in line right behind her.

"Hi," he says.

She points to her lips and shakes her head, then she waves and smiles.

After we put our things away, Mrs. Adler tells the students with special parts in the Fifth-Grade Sing to go to Mrs. Lineball's room for another re-hearsal. I still haven't come up with a good way to get out of it. Thermos gets up and walks away without waiting for the rest of us. Owen, Ryan, and I walk behind her down the hallway. Ahead of us I see a bunch of fifth graders from the other classes.

"Monday," Ryan whispers to us, "is Prank a Girl Day."

I roll my eyes. My stupid holiday is what started this whole thing. I don't think another holiday is going to make it better.

"Cool," says Owen.

"I'm not sure that's a great idea," I tell him. "That'll just start a war."

"So? It's already started." Ryan points to Thermos up ahead. "They started it."

I started it. But I don't know how to stop it.

When we get to her classroom, Mrs. Lineball divides us into groups based on the story or song we are doing in the show. There are a bunch of parent volunteers to help. Thermos and Ryan have to practice reading their piece together. Owen and a boy from another class read theirs with Owen's mom, but I have to work with Mrs. Lineball.

"Have you been practicing your song at home?"

I half nod, half shake my head. I haven't practiced, but I feel a little uncomfortable admitting it. "I just—I don't really—"

"Don't worry if you don't know every word yet. We still have over a week." Mrs. Lineball cuts me off before I can figure out how to tell her I don't want to do it. "The moment I chose *Free to Be . . . You and Me* for our sing, I just knew you'd be the perfect person to sing William's song."

"I'm not," I tell her. "Really."

"Mrs. Adler explained to me about your stage fright, but she also told me it's really improving. Your grandmother volunteered to help as well."

Just then, I see Grandma standing in the doorway of the music room talking on the phone. "I've got to go now," she says. She touches the screen, drops the phone into her giant black-and-pink purse, and walks over to where Mrs. Lineball and I are sitting by the piano.

"I'm sorry I am late." Grandma pulls a chair over.

"You are just in time. Louie and I were about to start."

Mrs. Lineball searches through a big pile on top of the piano, finds the right music, and plays the intro to the song. I sing it in the softest voice I can manage since I don't want the other kids to hear the first words. The words that tell everyone the song is about a "friend" named William. Everyone knows when you tell them something about your "friend" you really mean yourself.

"Can you try it a bit louder, Louie?" Mrs. Lineball asks.

I look over at Thermos and Ryan. They have to pretend they are texting each other while they say their lines. They have giant fake cardboard cell phones. I can hear pieces of their story, since they are not whispering. Ryan keeps telling Thermos she's not allowed to be on his baseball team, and Thermos keeps sarcastically congratulating him on his team's losses.

I could be louder if my song fit my personality.

"Let's try it again."

I start to sing the song as softly as I can once more, but then my grandmother starts singing with me. Actually, she's not singing. She's belting it. The other students and parents look over to this part of the room, so the only thing to do is sing a bit louder myself so my grandmother will stop. She does.

"Much better," Mrs. Lineball says. "Keep it up."

Mrs. Lineball goes to work with Owen and his partner and Grandma says, "The important thing in a song like this is to really think about the lyrics. *Feel* the story. You want everyone in the audience to root for William to have a doll."

I just don't want everyone in the audience to think *I* want a doll.

"Now sing it again," Grandma says.

Thermos and Ryan stop practicing and watch while my grandma swings her arms in front of me like she's conducting a one-person orchestra. I sing the part about the older brother making fun of William for wanting a doll and Ryan laughs. But Thermos chews on her thumbnail and squints her eyes at Ryan.

In my song everyone tells William he can't play with a doll because he is a boy. In Thermos's story, Ryan tells her character that she can't play baseball because she is a girl.

Weird, I think, as Grandma makes me sing the end of the song a second time. It's almost as if Thermos and I are doing the same part.

R-E-S-P-E-C-T

Saturday night at dinner, Grandma makes an announcement.

"I've got a movie for us to watch tonight."

Princess yips, and Grandma picks her up, kissing her all over her furry white face, leaving furry pink lipstick marks. It makes Princess look like she has patches of pink fur. "Yesh, even you, Prinshesh. Wanna watcha movie? Wanna?" I steal a look at Ari and we both smile. Grandma sounds kind of crazy when she talks in her Princess voice.

"What movie?" asks Ruby. "Is it *Musical Mermaid Palace*? Stinky Kate says nobody even likes unicorns anymore and mermaids are better."

Grandma shoots a look at my mom, who says,

"You can like whatever you want, sweetie. I bet lots of kids still like unicorns."

"This movie isn't about mermaids or unicorns. I thought it would be fun for us to watch *Free to Be . . . You and Me*."

Princess yips in excitement, and Ari says, "I love *Free to Be . . . You and Me*. I watched it at Emma's house once."

I try to blend in to my chair. Maybe if I am invisible they will watch it without me.

"I think watching the whole movie will really help you connect with your song, Louie." Grandma looks right at me. I don't think I blended enough.

"Actually, I was thinking of working on my video tonight," I tell her. "I've nearly gotten close to almost having an idea."

Mom gives me a look. "Grandma had to go to three different libraries to find a copy of *Free to Be . . . You and Me*. I think we'd better watch it with her."

I can tell from my mother's tone of voice that I don't have much choice. At least if Dad were here he'd probably suggest we have ice cream sundaes while we watch.

We help Ruby clear the table, which is totally unfair. She's plenty old enough to do it all by herself if you ask me. Then we head to the family room to watch the movie.

It starts with the song Mrs. Lineball taught us about running free in a special land with horses. Ari and my grandma sing along. I flop backward

on the floor. I don't know how I will be able to handle the entire hour. But when the song finishes, a little skit with puppets starts, and I recognize the voice of one of my favorite comedians, Mel Brooks. "Is that the guy from *Spaceballs*?" I ask Grandma.

She winks at me. "Uh-huh."

I sit up and pay closer attention. The skit is about two newborn babies who can't figure out if they are boys or girls. The boy thinks he is a girl because his feet are dainty and he wants to be a cocktail waitress when he grows up. The boy thinks the girl is a boy because she is bald and wants to be a firefighter. It's pretty funny.

When that skit is over, we watch a bunch more skits, and all of them are sort of about the same thing: boys and girls don't have to be exactly how everyone says they should be. Girls can like sports and be girls, and boys can hate sports and be boys. Some of the sketches are pretty funny.

But I still don't want to sing "William's Doll." I can kind of see what the song is saying: there is nothing wrong with a boy playing with a doll. The thing is, everyone but the grandma makes fun of the boy in the song and that's what will happen to me in real life if I sing it. Movies like *Free to Be . . . You and Me* might try to convince us that boys and girls can do and like anything, but I don't think everyone's buying it.

Although lots of fifth-grade girls play soccer or softball, Thermos is the only girl in our grade who seriously plays sports all the time, and even though she's the best, a lot of the boys won't play with her. And look at Ruby. Some kid in her grade doesn't want to play with her just because Ruby likes to hang out with Henry. Boys and girls can do and be whatever they want, but that doesn't mean the other kids will be okay with it.

But even more important, I don't know why Mrs. Lineball thought *I* should be the boy to sing "William's Doll." I don't know what the other kids will say or do when they hear me sing it. (Which actually they won't, because I plan to think of some way out of it.)

When the movie ends, Mom tells Ruby it's time to

take a bath, and Ari says she's going to do her *home-work*. That leaves me and Grandma sitting on the couch. I try to think of an excuse to disappear, fast, but Grandma's faster. "Let's work on your song."

"That's okay," I say. "I don't really want to."

Grandma frowns at me. "But you sing it so well, Louie."

I sigh. "I really wanted to talk to my dad."

Grandma purses her lips, but she doesn't try to convince me to practice anymore. She makes her *tsk* sound, but says, "Of course. Call him."

I turn on the computer and notice that I have an e-mail from Ryan Rakefield. I wonder if he decided to tease me online since he can't really get a rise out of me in person anymore. I open the e-mail:

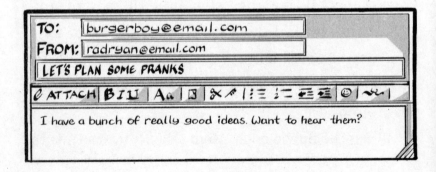

TO: burgerboy@email.com
FROM: radryan@email.com
LET'S PLAN SOME PRANKS

ATTACH B I U | A a | | | |

I have a bunch of really good ideas. Want to hear them?

I close the e-mail and run my hands up the back of my short-grass hair. I miss my curls. I miss Thermos. I miss *not* getting e-mails from Ryan Rakefield. I want to go back in time to before Thanksgiving when my life was the way I liked it.

I open the computer-chat program and call Dad. The little noise pings and pings and pings, but he doesn't answer. I remember what my dad said about chatting all the time. He shouldn't have said he could when he couldn't.

I turn off the computer and head to my room. I don't want to have a prank war with the girls, and I don't want to have a comedy war with Thermos, and I don't want to stand up in front of a million fifth graders and their parents and sing a song about playing with dolls, but I don't see a way out of any of it.

As I walk down the hallway, I hear Ruby splashing in the bathtub and asking my mom if she can get some mermaids.

"I'll have to see how much they cost," Mom says. "Maybe for Hanukkah. Or maybe Santa will bring them for Christmas. Are you sure you even like mermaids? What happened to unicorns?"

"Stinky Kate says they are for babies, and Grandma says I should be friends with Stinky Kate so she won't be so stinky anymore."

"Hmmm," says Mom.

Farther down the hall, I hear Grandma in Ari's bedroom singing the grandmother part from "William's Doll." Princess barks along like she's singing, too.

"Good shinging, Prinshesh! Good shinging!" Grandma coos.

When I pass by Ruby's room, Ari is sitting on the blow-up bed surrounded by all the makeup Grandma gave her. I poke my head in the door.

"You're a girl, right?" I ask.

Ari rolls her eyes at me.

"Okay, I know you're a girl. I just meant, can I ask you a question about that?"

Ari puts the mascara and tiny mirror she was holding down on the bed and says, "Oookaaay."

"Thermos is mad at me." I shove my hands in my pockets and rub my foot against the carpet.

"That's not a question." Ari picks up the tube of mascara again and twists off the cap.

"My question is why."

"Why?" Ari holds the little mirror in front of her eyeball with one hand and tries to run the mascara brush over her eyelashes with the other hand. It doesn't work. She keeps blinking her eye and winds up with black stripes all over her eyelid and cheeks. Finally she puts the mascara down, wipes her face with a tissue, and looks at me. "How could *I* tell you why? I don't even know what happened!"

"But you're a girl," I say again. "And nothing happened. So can you tell me why girls get mad at boys for no reason?"

Ari raises one eyebrow at me, like she's a detective who doesn't buy my alibi. "Well, the first thing you should know is that girls don't get mad at boys for no reason, so if Thermos is mad at you, she's definitely got a reason. And it's probably a really good one."

She squints at me with her detective eye again. "The main reason girls get mad at boys is that the boy *did* something stupid or *said* something stupid. I bet you know which you did."

I swallow. I think I *said* something stupid at first, but by now I've *done* a bunch of stupid things, too. "What if I don't want her to be mad at me anymore? And don't tell me to apologize. I already tried that and things only got worse."

"Girls want to know that you like them and that you respect them. You have to show her that you don't think the stuff she likes is dumb. You think it's cool and interesting and just as important as the stuff you like."

"But what if I don't like the stuff she likes?"

Ari dips a white triangle in some red powder and dabs it on her cheeks. It makes her look like she just ran a race. "You don't have to like her stuff. You just have to think it's cool that *she* likes it.

R-E-S-P-E-C-T. Haven't you ever heard Grandma sing that song?"

"I try to tune it out whenever Grandma sings." I say good night to Ari, then head to my room. I'm not sure if her advice makes any sense. I think Thermos is mad at me because I said she wasn't like a girl, but the stuff that she likes isn't what most girls like, so if I show her that I respect that she likes stuff that girls don't like, won't she get mad at me again?

I flop down on my bed and try to think of the things Thermos likes: sports, soup, jokes, scary books. She already knows I think those things are cool.

Then it hits me. I sit straight up on my bed. Thermos must also like being a girl, even if she doesn't act the way most of the other girls act. She got mad at me when I said she was like a boy. So she'll get un-mad at me if I tell her that I'm glad she's a girl.

But why would I be glad that she's a girl?

MAN OF THE HOUSE

On Sunday morning, I tell everyone that I get the computer to myself. I head into the family room with my comedy notebook and I ping my dad. When he answers, he's wide awake and there is no one around to ruin our talk. It's almost like male-bonding time.

"Hi, Louie!"

"Hi." I've got so many things I want to talk to my dad about I'm not sure where to start. I open my comedy notebook to the back page, where I made a list of questions:

- WHY DO ALL THE BOYS IN MY GRADE WANT TO GO OUT WITH GIRLS? HOW CAN YOU TELL IF YOU WANT TO GO OUT WITH ONE, TOO?
- WHY DOES GRANDMA HAVE TO BUTT INTO EVERYBODY'S BUSINESS?

"What's up?" Dad asks.

"The sky." I think I'm going to ask him about Grandma. That's probably the easiest.

"Listen, Louie," Dad says before I can get started. "I've got some bad news."

"Bad news?" My stomach clenches.

"This sculpture is taking a lot longer than I thought it would. I won't be home by this Friday. I might not even get home until next Tuesday, which would mean I'll have to miss the Fifth-Grade Sing."

"But you said two weeks!" All this time I've been doing what he asked, trying to be tough about the whole thing even though having him gone has been a big pain in the butt. I kept up my end of the bargain. It's not fair.

"I know. I keep having to apologize to you. This whole experience is so different from what I imagined. But that's what happens when you try something you've never done before. We're learning what works and what doesn't. It'll go much smoother the next time."

"The next time?" I gulp. What if Grandma winds up living with us forever?

"Don't worry. Nobody's booked me yet. But hopefully I'll get more jobs in the future, right?"

I can't tell Dad that I hope he doesn't get any more jobs. That would be mean. But I can't tell him I hope he *does* get more jobs. That would be lying. I rub my hand over my lips like I'm deep in thought.

"Enough about me." On the computer screen I can see Dad pick up his laptop and carry it over to his hotel bed. He lies down on his stomach and props himself up on his elbows. "Tell me what's been going on in your neck of the woods."

I swirl my pen along the edges of my paper and say, "It seems like every boy in my class is asking a girl to Go Out."

Dad nods thoughtfully, but it also kind of looks like he's trying not to smile. "So," he says, "do you want to ask someone to Go Steady?"

"It's not Go Steady." I roll my eyes. "It's Go Out, and no way!"

Dad clears his throat. "Well, Louie, if you don't want to Go Out with someone, you don't have to."

I cross my eyes and stick out my tongue. "I know that, Dad."

"I'm just saying," he says. "There will be plenty of time for that later. Fifth grade is the perfect time for friendship."

"Yeah, but what if a girl gets mad at you? How do you get her to be un-mad at you and be your friend again?"

"Well, you could try—" My dad starts offering me a suggestion, but gets cut off when Ari barges into the room.

"Dad, Mom is being so unfair!"

"It's my turn. Get out!" I tell her.

"You've been in here forever already," she says. "I need to talk to Dad."

My mother walks into the room. "Ari, Dad is not going to give you a different answer than me."

"You guys are making me the biggest loser in my

school." Ari squints her eyes at my mom. It's the angriest I've ever seen her.

Dad is patting his hands in the empty air and saying, "Settle down, everyone. Settle down."

"I'm supposed to be talking to Dad right now," I remind everyone. No one listens.

"You are too young to wear makeup *every* day. And it's not good for your skin either."

"Grandma says her makeup is made of minerals that are very good for my skin. And if the other girls get to wear it, then how can I be too young? I'm the same age as they are."

My mother sighs. "Enough. Both of you go do something else. I need to talk to your father right now."

Ari stomps off. "I'm wearing it in the house," she calls back over her shoulder.

My mother puts her hand on her forehead.

"I wasn't done," I tell her.

"Louie, I really need to talk to your dad, okay?"

"Fine," I say. I start walking back to my bedroom, and hear my mother say, "I know I couldn't do this without my mother, but she and I are very different kinds of moms."

That's true for sure, but what I need right now isn't two different kinds of moms, it's a dad. Only my dad is too busy with his job to be my dad right now. He's not going to help me get out of the Fifth-Grade Sing, or make up with Thermos, or even get an idea for a video. I guess that's what he meant when he said I'd have to be the man of the house. Whatever happens from here on out, I'm on my own.

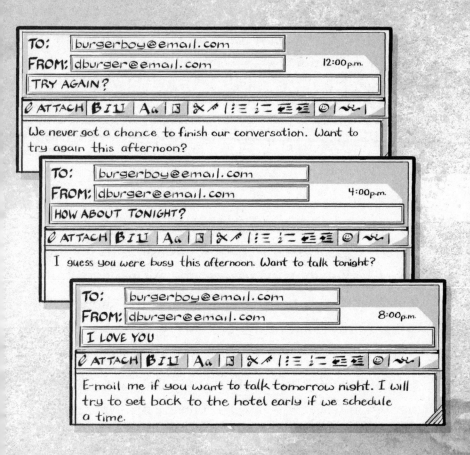

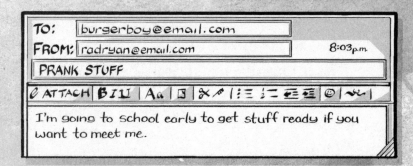

PRANK WAR

When Nick and I arrive at school on Monday, Ryan Rakefield runs to meet me at the edge of the blacktop. "You never e-mailed back. I thought of some really good pranks," he says.

I shake my head. I might have entered the twilight zone. Ryan is actually trying to have a conversation with me. One that doesn't involve teasing.

"I'm not sure," I tell Ryan. It doesn't feel right to work with him. To work against Thermos.

"Aren't pranks kind of mean?" Nick asks. "I don't want to be mean to Ava."

"Not all pranks are mean," I explain. "I've definitely seen pranks that are just fun. But I'm still not sure."

"Trust me," Ryan says. "My pranks are awe-some."

Nick and I give each other worried looks, but the bell rings and we have to go inside before Ryan can tell us what he's got planned. It doesn't take too long to find out. After social studies and silent reading, when Mrs. Adler tells us to line up for music, the girls all have *Boys Rule* signs taped to their backs. Ryan Rakefield catches my eye and smirks. Thermos catches my eye and scowls. My stomach wobbles.

Later, when we go to art, Ryan asks to use the bathroom and is gone for a very long time. I don't have a good feeling about it. At lunchtime, none of the girls have desserts in their lunches anymore, but the boys mysteriously have extra desserts. Ryan pops a cookie in his mouth and says, "Mmmm. This cookie is so good. How are your desserts, Louie?" I look at my lunch. In addition to the brownie my grandma made, I also have a Fruit Roll-Up. My mom doesn't buy Fruit Roll-Ups, but Thermos's mom does. Thermos gets one in her lunch most days.

I peek over at the girls' table, and Thermos and the girls are whispering and pointing at me. I get up, walk to their table, and offer them my brownie and the Fruit Roll-Up, but they ignore me.

At recess, I try to tell Ryan that I don't want to be part of the whole prank thing, but I can't find him anywhere on the playground.

At the end of the day, when the girls open their lockers to pack up, every one of them finds her locker filled with bits of shredded paper. The boys' lockers just have their coats and backpacks inside. Mrs. Adler has to bring two recycling bins into the hallway so the girls can clean up the mess. "Someone's been feeling mischievous today," she says, wrinkling her mouth at me.

I raise my eyebrows and point at my chest in the universal *Who, me?* gesture. I can't believe Mrs. Adler thinks I would prank everyone. But the girls are frowning at me as they carry armfuls of paper shreds from their lockers. Seriously, how did Ryan even have time to do all these pranks? I start picking up the paper that has fallen on the floor, and Nick does, too. Ryan makes a quick escape to the bus line, and Mrs. Adler tells the girls that they should catch the bus, too, if they ride one. Thermos and a couple other girls leave, but before she turns the corner of the hallway Thermos looks back at me and mouths the word *tomorrow*.

A shiver runs down my spine. I have a feeling I'm not going to enjoy tomorrow.

o o o

The next day we have music first thing, right after announcements, to get ready for the sing. Mrs. Lineball teaches us two more songs from *Free to Be . . . You and Me*. The first one is called "Sisters and Brothers." I can't help thinking that if I actually had sisters *and* brothers my life would be a lot simpler. There's a reason the song isn't called "Sisters and Even More Sisters." The second song is called "It's All Right to Cry." Ryan Rakefield makes pretend sniffles under his breath the whole time we sing it, so it's pretty clear that he doesn't actually think it is all right.

Then Mrs. Lineball invites me up to the front of the class. My stomach burbles. She didn't tell me I had to sing today.

"I know you're nervous"—Mrs. Lineball hands me a sheet of paper with the lyrics printed on it—"but we have to practice with the class singing the chorus."

She teaches them the line that begins with

"A doll, A doll," and instructs them to sing it in a teasing, taunting voice.

Then she plays the intro and nods at me when it's time to start singing. I can't see any way around it, so I sing. I sing about my "friend" who wants a doll. I'm sure that by the end of the day everyone will be asking me about my "friend" who likes dolls.

It's weird though. It doesn't seem like anyone is even paying attention to my words because as I sing, a humming noise fills the room. It is a very soft humming noise, so soft I'm not even sure if it's real or in my head, but from the way Mrs. Lineball and some of the boys look around the room, I think they must hear it, too.

Mrs. Lineball holds her hand up at me, so I stop singing and she stops playing the piano. When we are both silent, the room is silent, too. The humming noise is gone. Mrs. Lineball cocks her head and listens for another moment. The humming doesn't return, so she nods at me and starts playing again. The second I start singing, the humming comes back. It doesn't fit with the song, it's just one steady, annoying note like a lawnmower or buzzing telephone wires. I see a couple of girls looking at one another out of the corners of their eyes and smiling. Thermos smirks at me and shrugs her shoulders. I notice she keeps her lips pressed together.

When music is over, we go back to our regular class. It's time for social studies and when Mrs. Adler asks me to read the first paragraph of chapter four out loud, the hum returns. Mrs. Adler isn't fooled like Mrs. Lineball. She peers around the room and suggests that anyone in the mood to hum is welcome to return to Mrs. Lineball's music room.

There is no humming whenever anyone else reads, but every time I say anything it comes back. It's impossible to catch anyone doing it though. No one who's humming looks like they are humming. I *really* want to make up with Thermos. It's all I can think about for the rest of the day.

THE GREAT ESCAPE

The next morning Ryan passes out green stickers that say *Boys Rock!* to all the boys in our class. He sticks one on my chest, then lifts my arm up so he can give me a high five. "I've got even more pranks planned for today."

Nick and Jamal pull me aside and tell me we need to have a discussion.

They peel their *Boys Rock!* stickers off their coats and stuff them in their pockets.

"I want to ask Hannah to Go Out today," Jamal tells me.

I blink at him, confused. "That's fine with me," I say. "Go for it."

Nick shakes his head. "Ava says the girls took a

vote. No one is allowed to Go Out with any boys until the boys admit that girls rule. You've got to stop Ryan."

"I don't have any control over him! Why does everyone think we're in this together? I don't even like Ryan."

Nick looks at me sideways. "You told me you were e-mailing with him."

"I said he e-mailed me! I didn't e-mail him back."

"Well, you still have to do something."

"Why do I have to do something? And why do the boys have to say that girls rule, huh? Maybe the boys should make an agreement that none of us will Go Out with any of them until the girls say that boys rock."

Nick and Jamal look kind of uncomfortable.

"I don't know," Nick says.

I throw my hands up in the air. I don't want to be on Ryan's side, but sometimes girlzillas make it really hard to like them. Not *like* like them. Just like them.

After school, I try to propose a truce, but Thermos won't answer my phone calls or my e-mails. I e-mail Ryan to tell him I think we should end the prank war. But he thinks it is the greatest thing that ever happened at our school. He says the comedy showdown will be the cherry on top.

I worry the expression that might apply is: We're adding fuel to the fire.

o o o

By Thursday afternoon, comedy showdown time, I think I may have a plan. Unfortunately, it seems unlikely to work. Ryan told everyone who wants to watch to meet by the twirly slide on the third-grade playground. After the bell rings, Ryan heads to my locker and says, "Come on, Louie. Can't wait for you to crush it!"

"You go ahead," I tell him. "I've got to mentally prepare."

Thermos is at her locker next to me, and she snorts.

But there is nothing to snort at. I *do* need to mentally prepare. Just not for what she thinks.

Thermos starts to close her locker door, but I put my hand on her arm and whisper, "Wait."

She looks at my hand, then she looks in my eyes and I jerk my hand away, but say, "Please."

Thermos doesn't answer, but she doesn't close her locker.

"Are you coming?" Hannah calls to Thermos from the other end of the hall.

"I'll meet you out there," Thermos answers.

We stand silently side by side until the hallway is completely deserted. Then I say, "Quick! Follow me!"

I slam my locker and run the wrong way down the hallway, away from the playground. I hear footsteps behind me, so I think Thermos is following. I turn left, then right, until we are in the specials hall, and when we get to the music room I finally stop. Thermos nearly crashes into me.

"What are we doing?" she asks, sort of annoyed.

"I wanted to get out of our hall before anyone

came looking for us," I tell her. Then I knock on the music room door.

Mrs. Lineball opens the door. "There you are! Theodora, it is so nice of you to help Louie work on his song. I'll be right next door in my office if you need anything."

Thermos gives me a cockeyed look, but she doesn't say anything until Mrs. Lineball has left the room.

"Work on your song?" She puts her hands on her hips. "Are you doing another trick?"

"No! I promise. I wanted someplace we could talk, where we could escape from the comedy showdown and no one would see us. I made up an excuse so that Mrs. Lineball would let us use her room."

Mrs. Lineball peeks through the window of her office at us, so I give her a thumbs-up and sing the first line of my song.

Thermos looks back over her shoulder and smiles a great big smile that changes to a grimace as she turns back to me.

"What do we have to talk about? You've already

made it clear how you feel about girls. You hate them. Guess what? That means you hate me."

"You don't understand," I tell her. "You have it easy. Girls get to do whatever they want."

"What are you talking about?" Thermos shakes her head at me like I'm crazy.

"You can play sports or not play sports. Like at your football game, girls could choose to sit on the sidelines but I had to play."

"It's not that easy for girls to like sports, you know. Girls can play sports with other girls, but none of the boys wanted to let me play football with them when I first moved here."

"Well, what about hair?" I point out. "Girls can have any length hair, but as soon as a boy's hair gets too long people start telling him he looks like a girl."

"Hello? Plenty of boys have long hair. Just think about rock stars and skateboarders. Plus, I'm not allowed to wear my hair how I want it. My mom won't let me cut mine like Aunt Lisa's. Boys have it much easier!"

"No way," I say, and then I burst into song.

"What?"

"Mrs. Lineball. She was peeking in the room again."

"Oh." Thermos sits down in one of the music room chairs. "Boys are allowed to do disgusting things whenever they want. Nobody ever tells them they have to be ladylike."

"Girls don't have to pretend they won't miss their dad if he goes away. And they can yell and scream and make people listen to their problems if they want to. Nobody tells girls to be the man of the house." I sit down next to her.

"Yeah, well, nobody tells boys they have to wear a dress."

"I don't want to be in a war with the girls anymore. None of the boys do. Except Ryan. Can't we call a truce?"

"No more girls versus boys?"

I nod.

"Okay," she says. "But what about you and me?"

"You and me?" I gulp.

"Yeah," she says. "Do you have anything you need to say to me?" Thermos lifts her eyebrows expectantly.

I have no idea what she wants me to say. Suddenly I remember Hector and my question from Growing Up Night.

Oh no. She can't want—

"Are you two finished in here?" Mrs. Lineball

pokes her head in from her office. "I'm about ready to go home."

"Yep, we're done." I stand up and start walking to the door. Thermos doesn't follow right away.

"Are you coming?" I ask her.

She stares at me for a long time. Then she walks right past me and down the hall and out the front of the building.

The war between the boys and the girls? I'm pretty sure that's over.

The war between me and Thermos? That might not be over.

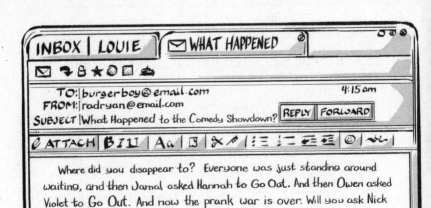

STINKY KATE

Friday is an almost normal day of school. There are no more pranks. The boys and girls are hardly talking to one another. (Not because they are fighting, but because they are all Going Out.) And Ryan decided to bug Jamal instead of me to ask Hannah to ask Thermos who she likes. Not that I want to know her answer, but I'm pretty sure it isn't Ryan.

At the end of the day, Mrs. Lineball comes into Mrs. Adler's classroom and they both remind us to practice our songs over the weekend. The Fifth-Grade Sing is Monday night. I'm going to spend a lot of time screaming this weekend. Maybe I will lose my voice by Monday.

When Nick and I go outside after the bell rings, only Henry is waiting for us on the first-grade blacktop.

"Where's Ruby?" I ask him.

"Your grandma picked her up," he says, frowning. "And Stinky Kate, too. I'm not allowed to play with them. Ruby says her grandma wants her to have more different kinds of friends."

Nick and I lock eyes with each other over the top of Henry's head as we start walking home. I've never seen Henry look so sad. In fact, I've never seen Henry look sad at all. He's usually Mr. Cheerful. "You can play with us today, Henry."

Nick doesn't look too thrilled about my idea, but I can't let Henry stay sad. I feel partly responsible since it was *my* grandma who said he couldn't play with Ruby today. "Want to help us make a video?"

"Are Ruby and Stinky Kate helping?" He sniffles, then wipes his nose on his jacket sleeve.

"Nope. Sorry."

That makes Henry look sadder, but he says, "Okay." Then he sighs.

When we get home, Ruby and Stinky Kate are sitting at the kitchen table having an after-school snack. The room smells like peanuts and cinnamon. Grandma made carrot muffins and apples with peanut butter and raisins.

"Let's eat our apples first, Ruby," says Stinky Kate. "We can pretend they are seaweed sandwiches. My mermaid name is Watella and your mermaid name is Fishina."

Ruby takes a big bite of her carrot muffin, but she doesn't say anything. Nick, Henry, and I sit down and Grandma gives each of us a muffin and an apple. "These muffins are delicious," Nick tells my grandma with crumbs spilling out of his mouth.

"Thank you." Grandma winks at Nick. "Now, I have to take a phone call in a few minutes," she tells us. "Ruby, you and Kate can play in your room. There is a big surprise in a box on your bed."

Kate turns to Ruby and puts her hand on Ruby's shoulder. "I'll open it, okay?"

Ruby looks at her lap.

"You can both open it together," Grandma says.

"We're going to go in the garage, okay, Grandma?" I clear my plate. "We want to work on my video."

Ruby's head snaps up. "Can we help?"

"I don't like to make videos," Kate says. "I want to play mermaids."

"I think it would be polite to let your guest choose the activity, Ruby," says Grandma. "You can help Louie another time."

Ruby and Kate clear their plates and head down

the hallway to Ruby's room. After they've been gone about a minute, I hear Stinky Kate shout, "Musical Mermaids! I thought you said you didn't have any."

Grandma smiles, then pushes a bunch of buttons on her phone.

"Ruby doesn't like mermaids," Henry whispers to me. "She likes unicorns."

"Come on, Henry. Let's go outside."

When we get to the Laff Shack, I pull out a notepad. "Let's brainstorm a list of ten possible videos," I say. "Then we will choose one and make it."

Henry walks over to the corner of the garage where Ruby's unicorn box is tucked under a small workbench Dad didn't take with him on his job. He gets out the unicorns and starts brushing and untangling all their manes. "We could play unicorns," says Henry.

Nick bulges his eyes at me, shakes his head, and waves his arms back and forth, saying no without letting Henry hear that he's saying no.

"Why don't you take care of the unicorns while Nick and I make the list?" I suggest.

Henry seems happy with that plan, so Nick and I sit down on the stage with my notebook between us.

"What about a silent video?" I tap my pencil against the side of my shoe. "It could be called *Silent but Deadly* and it would be about . . . you know."

Nick puts both hands up to his throat like he can't breathe. He crosses his eyes, then waves a hand in front of his nose. I put an asterisk next to *Silent but Deadly*. I think that one might have potential.

"How about a musical?" Nick bobs his head like he's listening to an imaginary song.

"I could call it *The Hound of Music*, and make it about a dog who thinks he can sing. Maybe I could even get Princess to star in it. She actually is a dog who thinks she can sing."

"I like it." Nick takes my pencil and puts an asterisk next to that idea, too. This might be my best idea day yet.

"Or maybe we could do a—"

Before I can finish my thought, Ruby comes

running into the garage, slamming the side door behind her. I'm so startled I practically fall off the edge of my stage. "Ruby? What are you doing here? Where's Kate?"

"Can I help you make a video? Stinky Kate is playing mermaids. I don't want to play mermaids, but Stinky Kate says she gets to be the boss of me because she is the guest."

I raise my eyebrows at Nick. This Kate kid seems like the bossiest person in the world. I wouldn't want to play with her either. But she is at our house, and Ruby can't just leave Kate alone to play mermaids by herself.

"Why don't you ask Kate to come in here with you?" I say.

Nick shakes his head and waves his arms back and forth again, but I believe the expression that applies here is: I can't just throw Ruby to the wolves. Even if it's only one wolf and the wolf is in first grade.

Ruby makes her hand into a fist and pumps her elbow up and down. "Yes!" She heads back to the side door of the garage, but it opens before she touches the doorknob.

"Look who I found in your room," Grandma says, leading Kate into the garage. "No, I want three hundred cases," she says into her phone. "Just a moment." Grandma turns back to Ruby and leans over. "Ruby, are you being a good hostess?"

"Louie said we could help make a video," Ruby replies.

Grandma stands up. "Three hundred of the red, not the plum!"

"I don't like making videos," Kate says.

"I know how to make it really fun," I tell her.

Grandma looks at Kate, then she looks at me uncertainly. "Are you sure?" she asks.

I give her a thumbs-up even though I'm really not sure, and having three first graders in my Laff Shack probably definitely means I'm not going to get any video-making done. Nick looks annoyed. Grandma scans the garage, then puts her phone to her ear and says, "Okay, read the entire order back to me," as she walks out the door.

When she's gone, Stinky Kate points a finger at Henry, who is quietly playing unicorns in the corner of the garage. "Unicorns are for babies," she says.

Henry freezes, one unicorn in each hand. He looks like he's not sure what to do next.

"They are not!" Nick stands up and furrows his brow at Kate. "I love unicorns."

Since Nick's on the stage and Kate is on the floor, he's about a thousand feet taller than she is. Plus, he's a fifth grader and she's only a first grader, but she doesn't seem scared of him.

"Yeah. I'm not a baby." Ruby stands next to Nick. "And Louie plays with unicorns, too."

I roll my eyes. I'd like to explain that I only play with them when I'm being nice to Ruby, but now isn't really the moment. Kate's face is turning red and her hands are balling up into little fists and her eyes are getting watery and shiny.

"It's true," Kate wails. "My mom and dad said!" Her voice wavers a little bit, and I think I better do something soon. I don't want Grandma coming back in here and thinking we've been torturing Stinky Kate.

"Hey, Kate," I say. "Do you go to music with Mrs. Lineball?"

Kate sniffles and says, "Uh-huh."

"She's teaching us a song called 'Mama Paquita,'" says Ruby.

"Mama, mama, Mama Paquita," Henry sings quietly while he prances a unicorn over his leg.

"She taught me a song, too," I tell Kate. "Want to hear it?"

Kate sniffles again. She doesn't nod her head, but she doesn't shake it no either. I take this as a yes.

"You sit right here," I tell Kate, directing her to one of the folding chairs in front of my stage. "I'm going to do a show for you. Ruby, you sit next to her."

"And can I make the video? I won't wobble at all very much."

This isn't really going to be my video, but I tell Ruby she can film it anyway. As long as I'm being nice right now, I might as well go all the way.

"Henry!" I call. "You come on up here. I need your help."

Henry starts walking over, but then I tell him, "Don't forget to bring your unicorns."

Henry looks excited when I tell him that. He grabs a bunch of them by the tails and carries them to the stage. I position him in the corner, then I ask Nick if he'll play the parts of the other boys, like the friend, the cousin, and the dad.

I teach Ruby and Kate the chorus of "William's Doll" and tell them to sing it whenever I point to them.

We practice a couple of times, and I grab a few items from my comedy supplies so that Nick can change costumes for each of his parts. I also dig through our sports bin so that I have the props the song mentions when the dad tries to get William to like sports instead of dolls.

When I'm sure that we have rehearsed enough, I tell Ruby to say "Action," and I start singing. This time it is clear that my "friend" who wants a doll really is a *friend* because you can see Henry sitting right next to me. Kate laughs when Nick sings the parts about dolls being for girls. My grandma walks in to check on us when we are halfway through, and I call her over with a toss of my head so she can sing the grandma part, which explains that William wants a doll so he'll know how to take care of a baby when he becomes a father someday.

When we finish Kate says, "That's not fair! I should have gotten to hold the camera. I'm the guest!"

Grandma stares down Stinky Kate. Then she says, "Only polite guests get to hold that camera."

I think Grandma may finally have seen the light about Stinky Kate.

"That was lovely, Louie!" Grandma says to me. "I can't wait to see you sing it at the Fifth-Grade Sing."

I wince at first, but suddenly I have a great idea. I don't believe it, but my grandma actually helped me think of a way to get out of singing at the show that will make everyone happy.

GRANDPAS ARE OKAY

After I e-mail with my dad, I send Mrs. Line-ball an e-mail with the link to the video I made. Ruby was right. Her filming was not wobbly at all, very much. She's improving. I ask Mrs. Lineball if we can show the video of the song instead of me singing live. That way no one will think I like to play with dolls. Except I don't tell her that last part. She e-mails back a yes right away.

I go to bed a little happier than last night because at least one of my problems might be solved. Now I just have to figure out what to do about Thermos.

o o o

When I wake up, I head to the kitchen, but stop right outside the doorway because I can hear Mom and Grandma talking.

"I was trying to be helpful," Grandma says. "You've had your hands full with work. It didn't seem necessary to bother you with every little question."

"I know, Mom," my mother says. "You've been very helpful, but David and I do things differently than you. So please, no more makeup for Ari, and Ruby doesn't have to play with anyone but Henry if she doesn't want to."

I hear a smacky sound, so I guess Grandma just gave Mom a kiss. "All you had to do was say so, dear."

A second later, Grandma dances past me singing more about pink Cadillacs driving down freeways of love. She pinches my cheek and kisses my forehead. I wipe it with the back of my hand and wonder where she's going.

In the kitchen, Mom is sitting at the table

drinking tea and reading a book. She has a big lipstick mark on her cheek.

"What do you want for breakfast?" she asks. "I'll make anything you like."

"Can I have cereal? Please? I haven't had cereal in two weeks."

"Sure." Mom laughs and starts to stand up.

"I'll make it! I haven't made my own food for two weeks either. Where's Grandma going? Did you kick her out?"

I put a bowl, a spoon, and a box of Rice Krispies on the table. Then I get the milk and sit down next to my mom.

"Louie! Of course I didn't kick her out. Grandma went to pick up Grandpa from the airport. He's flying in so that Grandma doesn't have to drive back to Michigan alone. They were going to leave tomorrow, but now they'll stay until your father returns."

I pour the cereal and then the milk and take a giant crackly bite. "When will that be?"

"Hopefully only a few more days." Mom takes

a big sip of her tea. She gives me a faint smile. "We've gone this long. We can manage."

"I miss Dad," I tell her.

Mom sighs. "Me, too."

Grandma and Grandpa return home around lunchtime. Grandpa brings lottery tickets for me and my sisters. We scratch them off right away, but none of us are winners. "Maybe next time," he says. "Who wants to watch the game with me?"

My mom and sisters say no, but Grandpa wraps his arm around my shoulder before I can give my answer. "Guess it's just you and me. It's great to have a football buddy."

I take a deep breath and lift my grandfather's arm from my shoulders. "Grandpa, you always bring good presents, but you and I see football differently. For you it's an exciting battle between warriors, for me it's a bunch of bobbleheads in funny pants running around in circles."

Grandpa frowns and lets his body sag. "You sure I can't convince you?"

I think about it for a second. "Nope. But I do like to play H-O-R-S-E. I play at school with Thermos. She really likes football, too. Only she doesn't like me very much right now."

"Girl trouble, huh?"

I put my hand on my forehead and shake my head. "That's all I've had for two straight weeks: girl trouble!"

Grandpa laughs, but then he suggests we play H-O-R-S-E, and while we do I tell him everything: Nick Going Out with Ava, Growing Up Night, Ryan Rakefield trying to be my friend, the prank war, Thermos getting mad, "William's Doll."

Grandpa is a really good listener. When I finish he says, "It sure is hard to grow up, isn't it?"

"I know!" I watch Grandpa take the shot I called. Standing on one foot to the left of the basket. It's my specialty. He misses.

"That's H-O-R," I say, catching his pass. "Girls have it way easier."

"Now, I'm not so sure about that," Grandpa says as I shoot my next basket. Backward, just in front

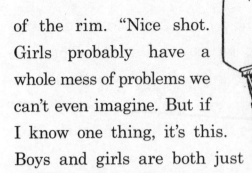

of the rim. "Nice shot. Girls probably have a whole mess of problems we can't even imagine. But if I know one thing, it's this. Boys and girls are both just people. They both have their challenges, but they both just want the same thing."

"Extra dessert?"

Grandpa shakes his head and chuckles. "Love," he says. "Love is what everyone wants."

I pretend to barf. "Gross!"

Grandpa wraps both arms around me and gives me an extra-long noogie. He smells like basketballs and aftershave, and I let my cheek rest against the fuzzy fabric of his sweatshirt.

Football might be torture, but my grandpa isn't so bad.

That night, I can't stop thinking about what Grandpa said, and suddenly brand-new lyrics to "William's Doll" pop in my head. I jump out of bed and write them in my comedy notebook before I forget them. Then I climb back into bed and wonder if Mrs. Lineball will let me change the show one more time.

MY FRIEND THERMOS

Mom drops me off at the Fifth-Grade Sing an hour before it's supposed to start. Mrs. Lineball approved my plan, but said I have to come in for an extra rehearsal right before the show. I meet her in the gym where the bleachers and piano from the music room are set up for our performance.

"I love your version of the song, Louie." Mrs. Lineball plays the intro and she doesn't have to tell me to sing in a louder voice because I sing it loud and clear. I just hope I'm not making a mistake. Otherwise Thermos will probably never be my friend again.

I sing the song for Mrs. Lineball two more times, and then the rest of the fifth graders start arriving so we stop rehearsing. I go stand in my place on the bleachers. As the auditorium fills with parents and grandparents and brothers and sisters, my stomach gets more and more antsy. I take a deep breath and shake out my hands like Mrs. Adler taught me, and I try to find one person in the crowd to focus on. That helps calm my stage-fright nerves. My eyes scan every row, but I don't see anyone I want to focus on. I see Thermos's parents, and her aunt Lisa and uncle Joe, but I definitely don't want to look at them during the show.

Finally I see Ari waving to me from the audience. I almost didn't recognize her because she isn't wearing any makeup and I forgot what her regular face

looks like. Ruby holds the video camera with Henry sitting next to her. I see Grandma, Grandpa, and Mom.

And Dad.

He made it!

Dad is standing right there with his arm around Mom's shoulder, giving her a kiss on the cheek. He turns to the stage, and when he sees me he makes Groucho Marx hands.

I make Groucho Marx eyebrows.

Someone at the back of the gym flicks the lights on and off and Mrs. Lineball asks everyone to sit down. Then she plays a few notes and the fifth graders sing "Free to Be . . . You and Me." Two kids

from another class do the baby skit and Owen tells a story about a boy who tipped over a sand table, but Thermos and Ryan really bring the house down when they do their skit about the boy who won't let the girl play baseball. When we've performed all our numbers but one, Mrs. Lineball stands back up to the microphone.

"For our last song, 'William's Doll,' a very enterprising student has made a video of the song and written his own extra verse. Without further ado, I present Louie Burger and 'William's Doll.'"

On the same big screen that Hector used for Growing Up Night, I watch the movie I made with Nick, Henry, Ruby, Kate, and Grandma. I hear Henry shout "That's me!" from the audience. When Grandma sings her lines, I know the video is almost over, so I step to the microphone. The lights come back up, Mrs. Lineball plays the intro, and I start to sing.

"When my friend Thermos was five or six, she wanted a ball to throw and kick. 'A ball,' said

Thermos, 'is so much fun. To bounce and toss and dribble and run.'"

I sing about how some people might think sports are for boys and art projects are for girls, but activities shouldn't be just for boys or girls. All kids should be able to do what they like no matter what, and nobody should say that somebody's not a boy or not a girl just because he or she acts a little different. My eyes scan the audience as I sing. Uncle Joe and Aunt Lisa sway and hold hands. Gross. My mother dabs at the corners of her eyes with her sleeve. Ryan Rakefield's dad folds his thick arms across his chest.

When I get to the end of the song, I look over at Thermos and say as loud as I can into the microphone, "Boys rock and girls rule!"

She pumps her fist in the air, so I do, too. Then all the fifth graders put their fists in the air. Ryan Rakefield even stands up and shouts, "Boys rock and girls rule!"

The audience gives us a standing ovation.

Mrs. Lineball claps so hard she knocks her sheet music onto the floor.

When the concert is over, I shove through the crowd as fast as I can, but when I get to the place my dad was sitting he isn't there anymore. I snake up and down the aisles and rows looking everywhere, but I don't see anyone from my family!

Then I hear someone call my name. I look around and see Thermos. She points to the front of the gym where my parents stand talking to Mrs. Lineball at the piano. I look back and forth between Thermos and my dad. I really want to talk to both of them and I can't decide who to talk to first.

Then Thermos points to my parents again, so I head over toward my family, but halfway there, Ryan Rakefield cuts me off.

I think today I will just ignore him, but he says, "I really liked your song."

Well, knock me over with a feather. That was a surprise. "Thanks."

Ryan scratches his throat with one finger. He looks like he wants to say something else to me, but he doesn't say anything. He almost looks nervous. I feel a little bad for him. Maybe if he isn't teasing, he doesn't know how to talk.

"You and Thermos did a good job," I say.

"Thanks," he says. "Uh, I really liked your song."

I'm about to joke and tell him that he and Thermos did a really good job again, but behind me I hear a voice shout, "Ryan! We're leaving!"

Ryan runs past me, and I see my dad standing at the end of the aisle, holding up his palms as if to say, *What are you waiting for?* I run to him and slam into his stomach.

"Oof," he says as he rubs my back hard and fast. I bury my face in his side and blink my eyes a bunch of times. His shirt must be kind of dusty. I'm not crying.

Well, maybe a little, but I don't know why. I'm not sad.

"You've got quite a boy there," Mrs. Lineball says

to my parents. "I just knew he'd be the perfect person to sing this song and really make it his own, but I had no idea he'd take it this far."

"*I* knew he'd be wonderful," says my grandma. "He's an original."

After we finish talking to Mrs. Lineball, Grandma says, "I believe it's traditional to go out for ice cream after a show like that."

"I could go for ice cream," Dad says. He's still got his arm around me, but I don't feel like squiggling away. Dad leans down and whispers in my ear, "We can have emergency male-bonding time tonight when we get back and I can finally help you with your problems."

At first I feel relieved, but then I realize I don't need to talk about those problems anymore. I don't want my dad to feel bad, though, so I say, "Have you ever heard of the book *A Father's Advice*? It was written by B. Goodson."

Dad smiles and says, "No, but I have heard of the book *Under the Bleachers* by Seymour Butz."

"I made a really good video," Ruby interrupts.

"It's called *Louie's Greatest Song by Louie.* Want to see it?"

"I do," I tell her. "Let's watch it at the ice cream shop."

When we get to Frosty House, it's packed full of kids from my school. Nick's family is there. They are sitting with Ava's family. Owen is there and Violet, too. And Thermos. She and her family are ordering at the counter.

We step in line behind them, and my whole body starts to feel cold and clammy.

Mrs. Albertson turns to me. She purses her lips and gives me a strange look. "Hello, Louie. That was an interesting song." She looks at my parents. "Good to see you again."

My parents say hello, but I don't say anything. My mouth is dry. I just want to know if Thermos hates me forever or not.

"I'm sorry I didn't tell you about the song before," I whisper to her. "Are you mad at me?"

I stand there for a second holding my breath before I realize Thermos is shaking her head no. She's not mad. My heart skitters in relief. "Really?"

Mrs. Albertson looks me up and down. I get the feeling she's listening to everything we are saying.

"Can Thermos and I go outside for a second?" I ask my parents.

"It's fine with me if it's okay with the Albertsons," my dad says.

"It's all right with us," Thermos's dad says.

"Just make sure you stand where we can see you," her mother adds.

Thermos and I head out the door. I remember to push this time, and the cheerful sound of bells trails outside into the cold after us.

"I hated being in a fight with you," I tell her. My breath comes out cloudy when I talk. "But I didn't know how to tell you that I like you exactly the way you are without you getting mad at me. I'm glad you don't do things exactly the way other girls do them, but if you wanted to I'd still be one of your best friends because no matter what, you are the coolest girl in fifth grade."

Thermos wrinkles her lips, then twitches them from side to side. "Okay."

"Seriously?"

She nods. "Uh-huh."

"Friends again?"

Thermos punches me in the arm. "Best friends."

MY FRIEND THERMOS
(SUNG TO THE TUNE OF WILLIAM'S DOLL)
by Louie Burger

WHEN MY FRIEND THERMOS WAS FIVE OR SIX,
    SHE WANTED A BALL TO THROW AND KICK.
"A BALL," SAID THERMOS, "IS SO MUCH FUN.
    TO BOUNCE AND TOSS AND DRIBBLE AND RUN.
A BALL TO SHOOT INTO A HOOP,
    I'LL PLAY ALONE OR WITH A GROUP.
A BALL THAT'S GIANT OR THAT'S SMALL,
I'LL BOUNCE THEM ALL AGAINST THE WALL."

A BALL, A BALL, THERMOS WANTS A BALL.
"GIRLS DON'T PLAY SPORTS," SAID HER
    BEST FRIEND LOU.
"WHY WOULD A GIRL WANT TO PLAY WITH A BALL?"
LOU THOUGHT AND THOUGHT,
    TILL HE THOUGHT HE KNEW.

"I WAS A JERK," SAID HER WISER FRIE-END.
"WILL YOU PLEASE FORGIVE ME,
    SO OUR FRIENDSHIP CAN ME-END?"

A GIRL IS A GIRL, NO MATTER HER THING.
SPORTS OR ART OR WINDING UP STRING.
A BOY'S A BOY IN THE SAME WAY,
NO MATTER THE GAMES HE LIKES TO PLAY.
BECAUSE EVERY GIRL AND BOY
DESERVES A HOBBY THEY ENJOY.
THERE'S NO ONE WAY THEY ALL SHOULD BE,
EXCEPT FOR BEING HAPPY.
    I'M SURE THAT WE CAN ALL AGREE.

A BALL, A BALL, THERMOS WANTS A BALL.

A STAGE, A STAGE, LOUIE WANTS A STAGE.

A SANDWICH, A SANDWICH, NICK WANTS A SANDWICH.

A BEAT, A BEAT, JAMAL WANTS A BEAT.

A UNICORN, A UNICORN, RUBY WANTS A UNICORN.

MASCARA, MASCARA, ARI WANTS MASCARA.

RUBY, RUBY, HENRY WANTS RUBY.

A PRANK WAR, A PRANK WAR, RYAN WANTS A PRANK WAR.